TCC Te

2o2

Congratulations!

It's Raining in Moscow and I Forgot My Umbrella

Caroline Boxall

It's Raining in Moscow and I Forgot My Umbrella

Caroline Boxall

First published 2020
Box of Books Publishing

This is a work of fiction. Names, characters,
places and incidents are either the product of the
author's imagination or, if not, are used fictitiously

Caroline Boxall asserts the moral right to be
identified as the author of this work

Front cover by Graham Smith Design

ISBN: 978-1-8382388-1-0

Dedication

For Boxy, Megan, Beth, Emily, Katie and
Charlie

And for my mum

Acknowledgements

Thanks to my wonderful family who encouraged me all the way and gave me so much material by being themselves.

To my mum. Only a mother would read every draft of a book as many times as she did – and enjoy it each time!

To Louis who gave me endless, patient advice about life as a firefighter and for climbing that tree.

To Graham for designing the spectacular book cover in record time.

To Grandma and all dementia sufferers everywhere for inspiring me to write this book.

It's Raining in Moscow and I Forgot My Umbrella

Prologue

England - nine years ago

"What have I done?"

The Russian girl sat by the edge of the road, twisting car keys round and round her fingers, watching fearfully as the flames lit up the night sky. Lights in the other houses were gradually bringing the tiny village to life; the residents woken by the noise of the fire engine, the shouting and the roaring blaze itself. Some were watching in shocked fascination from the safety of their homes, but others were rushing out to help.

A frail, elderly lady had already been carried from the burning house, and now the girl looked on in horror as a second firefighter emerged from the blazing building, carrying a small boy.

"I didn't know, I didn't know," she trembled, and hugged her knees closer, rocking backwards and forwards.

As the firefighter gently passed the child to the paramedics, the little boy turned his head. It seemed, to the girl, that he was looking straight at her. The girl shivered involuntarily, despite the heat from the fire.

An explosion inside the house brought the girl

back to her senses and she became aware of a new sound drawing closer and growing louder. Police sirens! She jumped into the driver's seat of the old Ford Fiesta and started the engine. Her car disappeared over the hill, into the blackness, just as the police arrived.

Everything could have been so very different if she had found the courage to stay.

Chapter One

England - the present

I knew they were following me.

I could feel it in the back of my neck and forced myself not to turn round. The most important thing was not to let them follow me home. My instinct was telling me to turn right, but I wasn't about to let them see where I live, so I turned left out of the school gates.

The drizzle was making me blink, and the sky was already dark from the thick grey clouds. Cars were rushing past with their lights blinding me and their wheels spraying oily water.

"Billy," called Jude's voice. "Billy, we're coming for you!"

It had started at lunchtime. The whole class was lining up in the corridor, waiting to go into the dining-room and I was reading a new poster on the wall which said,

"Can you help find these missing persons?"

It was about teenagers who had disappeared, and the reasons why they might have vanished. I don't like seeing photos of missing people, but it helps to know I'm not the only person to have lost someone.

While I was studying the poster, I didn't notice the queue had moved forwards and Jude, who was behind, gave me a massive push. I was caught off balance and fell over. Mrs Beaman had seen the whole thing and sent Jude to the back of the line.

In the lunch queue Jude walked past me with his tray of sausage and mash.

"I'm gonna get you for that, Billy. You'd better watch out," he hissed.

"You've got it coming." whispered Tyrone.

Slobbery Big Ben was close behind, trying to balance his enormous pile of food.

"Gonna getcha!" he spat, slobber bursting from his colossal mouth and dropping at least four sausages off his tray. As he bent down to pick them up, he managed to tip all his food onto the floor. He didn't seem to care, and he scooped the whole lot off the floor, back onto his tray, and licked his hands.

You don't have to do much to get on the wrong side of Jude, and now, on the narrow pavement outside school, I started thinking about what he might do to me. The black bars of the school railings were making me feel dizzy as I walked past, and I could hear someone behind me pulling a stick against the bars, making a jangling noise. I pulled my rucksack closer to my back as if it

4

might give me some protection. The rain was getting heavier and the car lights were getting brighter. I began to wish I'd headed for home after all

"We're coming for you!" I heard Big Ben's voice behind me.

I wasn't worried about Big Ben. He's huge but he doesn't have much pace and I can easily outrun him. Tyrone is the strong one, always talking about how much protein he needs for his muscles, and about his dad who used to be a boxer. I'm pretty sure one punch from Tyrone would knock me out.

"We're right behind you," came Tyrone's deep voice. "And we're getting closer..."

I tried really hard not to show it, but I was terrified, especially as there wasn't anyone else from school around. At any moment I expected a smash on the head or an arm lock, but they were enjoying freaking me out by just keeping a little bit behind.

"Are you ready for it?" came Jude's voice. I thought about crossing the road but there was too much traffic and it was already getting dark. I'd never make it to the other side.

I started taking longer and quicker strides and I could feel my heart beating. If I could get to the park there might be somewhere to hide. The temptation to turn round suddenly became too much for me and I looked behind. Just as expected, there was Jude in front with his hood pulled over his head. Slightly behind I could see Tyrone, his black puffa jacket making him even wider than usual, and behind him, at least a head taller than the others, was slobbery Big Ben, his mouth wide open in a lopsided grin.

"Let's get him!" shouted Jude, and they started running at me.

I ran towards the park gates. They were shut! Now what? There was a woman in front of me with a wide buggy, a thick hedge to the left, the gang behind me and the busy road to my right. I only had one choice. As I stepped into the road, the roar of traffic pounded in my ears, followed by the screeching of tyres. I shut my eyes and waited for the impact...

Chapter Two

Russia - sixteen years ago

Manya stood on the podium in the Great Hall listening to the applause.

Highest academic achievement. The other students were sitting up straight in their chairs, clapping dutifully, little grimaces on their faces. Manya had won the school's most prestigious prize and they were struggling not to reveal their contempt.

Manya wasn't interested in the other pupils. She didn't care what they thought or whether they were jealous. She deserved to win. She looked over to the only person who was genuinely pleased about her prize, her father. Mr Molchalin was ecstatic. He had always known Manya would do well and she had surpassed all expectations. He glanced over at his wife with her stony face barely concealing that ever-present, unforgiving expression. He sighed. He would not let her ruin this moment. He looked back at his daughter.

Manya's gaze had switched from her father to her mother. Mrs Molchalin was wearing her smart grey suit with the fox-fur collar, her black hair was scraped back tightly, and her red lipstick glistened against her pale skin. She was not looking at her daughter and her face confirmed what Manya already knew. She would never earn her mother's approval. She remembered her Grandmother, Babushka's words:

"Manya there is nothing you can do about it; your mother will never forgive you. You need to be strong. You can do anything you set your mind to and remember, I will always be proud of you."

Thinking about Babushka brought tears to Manya's eyes and she looked down.

I will not show emotion. I am strong. I can do anything, she silently chanted.

She thought about how her prize would almost certainly guarantee her place at Pushkin Academy. From there she might even move on to study at the great Moscow State University, the best university in Russia. Her degree would ensure a fabulous job and she would become totally independent. She would not have to rely on anybody but herself. She raised her eyes again to the sea of faces, sour and unfriendly. She didn't need any of them.

It was the custom for parents to take their children out for tea in the nearby town after the prize-giving ceremony. Manya had begged her father not to go but he had insisted.

"Why not?" he had asked, "I have the

cleverest, most accomplished daughter in the whole school, and I want to show her off. I want everyone to see that I, Dmitri Molchalin, am the father of a child prodigy. You never know who might be taking tea at the next table. There are some very influential families at your school, Manya. We mustn't miss any opportunities."

So Manya found herself sitting between her parents in the most expensive tearoom in Smolensk. A three-tiered cake tray sat on the table in front of her, heaving with tiny sandwiches, honey cakes and chocolate eclairs. Manya couldn't eat; she sat with her hands folded together on the navy skirt of her neatly pressed uniform. Her tight blazer was too hot, but her father would not allow her to remove it. He too was clearly struggling in his thick dark suit. She could see beads of sweat forming at the top of his forehead and his neck was reddening above the white starched collar of his shirt. Mr Molchalin was systematically working his way around the cake tray. Manya wondered how there was room for the great gulps of food to fit past his tightly bound throat.

Her mother was wearing her absent expression and remained silent throughout. Her father spoke constantly.

"Manya, I have told you before that my investment in your education has always been about the contacts. If you look over there you will see Mr Kozlov – he practically runs Russian Railways. Is his daughter in your class?"

Manya remained silent. She didn't look over to the Kozlov table. She knew Alena Kozlov. Alena had tried to befriend Manya last year, but Manya didn't want to be friends with anyone. She couldn't see the point in having friends. Other girls had friends and they either argued with each other or gossiped about each other. Why would Manya want a friend? So she had told Alena she had a highly contagious skin condition, and it would be better for Alena to keep her distance. It had worked.

"And what about Dr Orlov? Do you know his daughter?"

Manya shook her head. Izabel Orlov had once tried to copy Manya's work during a test and, when she realised, Manya had produced a dramatic yawn. She had stretched her arms widely and strategically.

"Gosh, Izabel," Manya had cried, "I didn't see that glass of water on your desk right next to your paper!" Manya had gone back to her test as Izabel tried to salvage what was left of her paper which now looked more like an art project.

The tearoom hummed with low voices and tinkling teacups. Her father's voice broke in once more.

"So, Manya Molchalin," he said, loudly enough for everyone in the tearoom to hear. "Now that you have won all the prizes, you will most likely be accepted at Pushkin, the school for the gifted and talented," he added, his voice increasing in volume. Manya cringed and looked at the floor. Some of the other families turned briefly to look at the Molchalin family. None of them smiled.

Chapter Three

England - the present

As the tyres screeched towards me, I suddenly felt a strong hand grab hold of my arm and pull me out of the road. I was swung across the path and found myself face down in a wet bush. I didn't mind the water dripping down my neck, but the bush was prickly, and it felt like my face was being pressed into a hedgehog. I twisted my head to see who had pulled me out of the road, and perhaps saved my life. I could make out the back of a figure dressed entirely in black with a hood. This person, whoever it was, had turned to face Jude and the others. The stranger must have been using strong language because I watched Jude's face crumple. Big Ben's slobber had increased in volume and was bouncing up and down like a slimy yoyo. I couldn't hear what had been said above the roar of the traffic, but it was clear that the three boys had changed their minds about chasing me. They turned round and ran in the opposite direction. I twisted my neck further to see who the dark figure was, but at that moment a pair of brown trousers got in the way.

"Are you alright? What were you doing stepping into a busy road? I nearly ran you over!"

The man wearing the brown trousers pulled me out of the bush. I tried to look past him because I wanted to see who had scared off the gang, but nobody was there. Not even Jude.

"Are you okay?" the man repeated.

There was a queue of traffic building up. He must have been the driver of the car with the screeching tyres.

"Yes," I stammered, "I'm really sorry, I didn't realise there was so much traffic. I'm fine. Thanks for not to running me over."

The man shook his head and went back round to the driver's door. "Watch where you're going next time," he muttered.

I stood for a moment thinking about the last couple of minutes. Who was that mysterious figure in black? I wanted to know what had been said to Jude to make him run away. I hadn't even been able to say thank you.

I decided to get home as quickly as possible. I didn't want Neelam to worry or even to wonder where I'd been.

"*It's fine Neelam,*" I'd say. "*I was chased by the grisly gang who tried to attack me with bouncing slobber. I ran into the road and was nearly mashed by a Volvo, but a stranger saved my life by chucking me into a prickly bush.*"

No. Neelam has enough worries without adding my walk from school to her list. I was just relieved that Jude hadn't followed me home because where I live isn't exactly normal, and I don't want him to know.

Chapter Four

Russia – sixteen and a half years ago

Mr Molchalin had taken Manya to Moscow to look around Pushkin Academy a few months before the prize ceremony. Manya had never been to Moscow before and she wasn't sure if she wanted to live so far from home. Her lack of enthusiasm had irritated her father on the long drive to Moscow. They spent most of the journey in silence, each deep in their own, very different thoughts.

Mr Molchalin wanted his daughter to impress the teachers. He desperately hoped she would behave well, especially in front of the head teacher. He needed her to put on her smiling face rather than the current sulky one. Appearances were important to him and he had carefully selected both his own dark suit, and Manya's blue and white dress with matching shoes. It didn't occur to him that his daughter might have other needs. To him the road to accomplishment and prosperity was the same as the road to happiness. They were one and the same thing.

Manya had other thoughts on her mind. She liked being the best. A school for 'Russia's Gifted and Talented' would surely select students who were at least as intelligent as herself. Would she be able to deal with the competition? Would she still win prizes and make her father proud?

His voice interrupted her thoughts.

"Did I tell you about the brand-new athletics track at Pushkin?" he asked.

"Yes Papa. I can't wait," said Manya in a dull, bored tone. "You know how much I love running."

"And they have an interactive sand box where you can learn about rivers."

"Cool," she said in the same flat tone, "I should have packed my bucket and spade."

"And a new ICT suite."

"New?" exclaimed Manya, suddenly alert.

"The prospectus is on the back seat. Take a look."

Manya opened the glossy brochure and flicked through until she found the photo of a brightly lit room filled with shiny silver computers, modems and printers. She read aloud,

"Computer science at Pushkin focuses on programming, verification and implementation."

Manya wasn't sure what all this meant but the words sounded fascinating. Anything to do with technology sounded good to her.

She remembered how, when she was twelve, her school had introduced ICT as a new subject. Mr Stepanov, the teacher, had enthusiastically set up an after-school Computer Club for anyone wanting to learn more than he was able to teach during the lessons. Manya had signed up immediately and Mr Stepanov had started to explain the basics of coding. But then she came third in a Russian language test and her father had been furious.

"What is this?" he had shouted, "Third? You only came third? Second is bad enough but Manya, I don't ever want to see you fail again. You will spend two hours every day after school studying the workings of our beautiful language."

"But Papa, I am working on a computer project after school!" Manya had protested.

"Not anymore. From tomorrow you will come straight home after school."

Well, Papa, thought Manya, sitting silently next to her father in the car, *you won't be able to stop me going to the ICT Suite if you're not there! You won't even know!* And she smiled to herself.

Her smile faded quickly as her thoughts turned to the other person she wouldn't miss if she went to boarding school: her mother. Mrs Molchalin was not in the slightest bit interested in her daughter. It was Babushka who looked after her, played with her and taught her how to cook. Her mother sometimes appeared from her bedroom at mealtimes but only if Mr Molchalin was also present, and she always behaved as though Manya wasn't there.

On her seventh birthday, Babushka had allowed Manya to invite her friend Sacha to come home with her after school. Mrs Molchalin had swept down the stairs, shouted at Babushka and stormed out of the house yelling, "I will return in ten minutes. There are to be no children in my house when I get back!"

Manya had been mortified. Babushka had tried to persuade Sacha to stay, but Sacha was terrified and had gone home. Manya had fled to her room and stayed there for the rest of the evening.

The following day, at school, Sacha announced that she didn't want to be friends with Manya anymore. Manya began to build up a little wall of protection around herself. The more she avoided the other children at school, the more they avoided her. She became more and more studious and this pleased her father enormously.

In the car Manya suddenly came to a conclusion: being at Pushkin would release her from her father's constant pressure and on top of that she wouldn't have to see her mother.

She glanced over at her father in the driver's seat next to her.

"Papa," she said, "I think this will be a very good school. Thank you for taking me, I will try my best to impress the teachers."

Mr Molchalin smiled and breathed a sigh of relief. "Manya, it is a great honour to visit this school. If you are offered a place to study at Pushkin, I will be very pleased and very proud of you."

Chapter Five

England - the present

I don't live in a house. Or a flat, a bungalow, a caravan, a palace or a hut. I live in an old people's home and I don't want anyone to know.

It was still raining, and I was very wet; my encounter with the prickly bush hadn't helped. I walked back past school and back home, taking extra care when I crossed roads. I'd had a close encounter with the front bumper of a Volvo, and it had shaken me up a bit. When I arrived, there were a few people chatting in the car park, probably visitors. We have lots of visitors.

By the time I walked through the parking area, my heartbeat had returned to normal. I looked up at the massive building, my home, and at the big slate sign with the words, "Autumn Days Care Home". I was glad Neelam wouldn't need to find out what had happened. She's always worried about me. She says just because she's not my real mum it doesn't mean she doesn't care. I'm lucky really. Well, I'm not lucky that I don't have a mum or dad but I'm lucky to have Neelam.

I pressed the code that lets me in through the big brown front door. The warm air hit me along with the familiar smell of washing powder and the sound of Elvis Presley who greeted me with, 'You ain't nothin' but a hound dog'. I like this room with its grand piano, its tall windows and all the tables surrounded by armchairs. I like seeing the ladies taking round the cake trolley and I like the cakes. I waved to the Oldies who were having a cup of tea. I call them Oldies because that's what they are. It's not meant to be rude.

"Hello Billy, how was school?" called the Oldies.

"Fine thanks!" I shouted back but then I ran up the stairs to the top floor to see Gran.

The top floor is the dementia floor, where everyone forgets things. They get their words muddled up and they can't do all the things they used to be able to do. At Autumn Days they don't call it the dementia floor, they call it "Nostalgia" which is supposed to sound more friendly.

There was Gran in her big blue armchair with the squashy cushions, her feet on a little stool playing with her doll. Gran loves her doll, it's called Dardar. Gran thinks her doll is real and she talks to it. In fact she talks to Dardar more than she talks to anyone else. I can't see why she's so keen on Dardar – the doll is hideous! It wears a pink frilly dress and has legs which are all bendy. It has tiny, scrunched up eyes and fat brown lips. It used to have hair but most of it's

21

fallen out. Probably from Gran brushing it too much. I sometimes have to talk to Gran through Dardar.

"Hello Gran," I said. "Hello Dardar. Dardar could you tell Gran that Billy has been to school and got two stars for maths."

Gran lifted Dardar's mouth to her ear and pretended to listen. Then she smiled at me and said, "I've just got back from flip flap, ooh it was so lovely, but there were ever so many pingle woodles and there wasn't any room for my elephant!"

It's great when Gran talks like that – we have a really funny chat sometimes. People might think it's sad I can't have a proper conversation with Gran. I never really know what she's saying but I make a good guess. If someone says they can't understand her she gets a bit upset.

I looked round at my other friends. I waved to Beryl.

"Have you got a girlfriend yet?" She says it every day and then laughs as if she's made the funniest joke. "Don't make me laugh," she always laughs, "you'll make me get wrinkles!" and that sets her off again.

Sometimes I go and have a chat with Beryl, but I noticed Frank looking at me. He seemed a bit worried.

"Billy you're late, where have you been?"

Frank is ninety-five and he's smart. I don't know why he's on the dementia floor because he remembers everything.

"I had to stay behind to talk to my teacher," I semi-lied. I don't like lying to Frank because he always notices. He used to be in the army.

"You weren't talking to your teacher were you?" he said. "You've got leaves all over your back and scratches all over your face. Has someone pushed you into a hedge?"

I remembered the figure in black who'd pulled me out of the road. I still hadn't worked out who it could have been. Was it Louis?

Luckily Neelam came over.

"Billy, have you had a good day? Mandy's just got back. Go and ask her for some cake before this lot eat it all up."

I went to get some cake. Mandy makes fantastic cakes and this one was just what I needed.

She asked if I wanted a slice of her 'lemon dribble' cake. Mandy often mixes her words up, but I didn't like to correct her. Dribble cake! It reminded me of Big Ben.

I ate the cake and went to my room to see if I could get rid of the bits of hedge before Frank questioned me again. Gran and I have our own bedrooms next to each other and Neelam's flat is on the opposite side of the corridor. When I was little, she let me take my railway track into her flat and when I had enough pieces, I set it out all the way down the corridors. There are lots of corridors on the Nostalgia floor with rooms on either side. It's a bit like a maze. There's a laundry, a post room, and a hairdresser. And there's a memory room where the Oldies can look at photos, wedding dresses and old kitchen equipment. It's supposed to help them remember things from when they were younger and give them something to talk about. The Nostalgia floor would be a great place to play hide and seek but I can't really do that because whoever I was playing with would forget what they were doing. I could be hiding for hours!

My room's quite big and I have a football pitch on my duvet. My walls are covered with Spurs players and I have six Spurs calendars, all from Beryl.

"You can put one up in your room and I'll look after the rest for you," she said. I went into her room the other day and the extra five calendars were hanging on her wall, all open at different months. I think she probably supports Spurs too. Either that or she likes looking at the players.

I'd like to watch football matches on the big TV in the lounge but it's usually showing old films like *Singin' in the Rain*, *Mary Poppins* or *Chitty Chitty Bang Bang* and I've seen them so many times I know them off by heart. On the dementia floor they forget they saw the same film the day before, so it doesn't matter. Strangely they can remember things from a long time ago and every time 'Singing in the Rain' comes on, Beryl says, "Ooh, I love that film. When I was nursing, I saw that one at the pictures (*that's Oldie speak for cinema*). That Gene Kelly was such a dish (*Oldie speak for good-looking*) and all us nurses dreamed of dancing with him!"

Chapter Six

Russia- sixteen and a half years ago

Manya loved Pushkin Academy from the moment she stepped into the large entrance hall with its flat panel display screens showing different parts of the school. She and her father had been shown around by a tall, serious-looking student. Manya had never seen such modern buildings, so many interactive whiteboards, so many computers! The prospectus had not been lying about the ICT Suite - it was magnificent. Rows and rows of gleaming machines, all beckoning Manya to turn them on. She walked around the room gazing at the blank screens, daring to touch a silver keyboard as she passed. She felt at home. These precision instruments may not love her any more than people loved her, but she would certainly love them.

"And these are the study bedrooms," said the serious-looking student. "Every pupil has their own room with a bed and a desk area with a laptop."

My own laptop! thought Manya. *One I can use whenever I like and experiment on without anybody looking over my shoulder saying, "that's not the way to do it."*

The drive to Moscow had been silent, but the way home was all talk. Manya told her father every detail of what she had seen over and over as if he hadn't been there. Mr Molchalin didn't mind. He knew that once his daughter had set her heart on Pushkin, she would do whatever it took to secure her place.

When they got back from Moscow, Manya went straight to her room and wrote herself a timetable to make sure she could fit in extra hours of study every morning and every evening in the weeks leading up to the end of year exams. It had paid off. She won the academic prize and an offer from Pushkin.

A few days before she was to leave for her new school in Moscow, Manya was sitting in her bedroom looking at the photo of her grandmother.

"If only you were still here," Manya said to the photo. "What would you say about my new school? Would you have been excited for me or would you have missed your Myshka, your little mouse?"

Manya thought back to the days just before her award ceremony, when Babushka had suddenly become very ill. Manya had sat next to her grandmother's rocking chair, talking to her, reading to her, or just holding her hand.

One morning, as they were sitting in silence, with the sun streaming through the window,

Babushka had suddenly let out a sob. Manya had been afraid and asked if she needed a drink. Babushka had leaned forward and clasped Manya's tight fists between her own, gnarled hands. She was holding her dragonfly brooch.

"I want you to have this. When you wear it remember me."

"No, Babushka…" Manya protested, but the old lady shook her head to silence her and continued.

"Manya, I have to tell you about your mama. I should have told you years ago, but I could never find the words. I should have seen something was wrong with her when she was a child. As her mother, I should have done something before it was too late. Now I can only ask for your forgiveness."

Manya's fear intensified. Babushka's breathing was shallow and gasping but she didn't call her father, she wanted to hear Babushka's story.

"Babushka, whatever it is I forgive you. Please tell me the truth," begged Manya.

Babushka's watery blue eyes fixed on the arm of the rocking chair and she began.

"When your mama was a child she played with dolls. She had twelve dolls, and she looked after them as though they were real children. Six boys and six girls. They all had names, their own clothes, birthdays, habits and characters. Your mama took them everywhere with her. She fed them, bathed them and put them to bed every evening. To begin with I thought it was a sweet game for a girl to play and I encouraged it. I made more clothes for the dolls and I even bought her a big pram so she could push them around.

"But Babushka," interrupted Manya, "that does sound normal for a little girl."

"That's what I thought," replied her grandmother. "But it was the beginnings of an obsession that got out of control.

"One day when she was about eleven, she told me she was 'preparing for the real thing'. That she was going to have twelve real children of her own. All this play was actually a rehearsal."

"Did she really want twelve children?" asked Manya, incredulously. She had always believed her mother didn't even like children.

"Oh yes," answered Babushka, sadly. "The Motherland is very proud of women who have many children; it is seen as a wonderful achievement. Even when your mama became a teenager she was still caring for her dolls as if they were real children. It didn't surprise me when she married at eighteen and was expecting her first child before her nineteenth birthday. She was convinced she was having a boy because her oldest doll had been a boy named Ivan.

"There were complications during the birth. At one point, your mama and the baby were both in danger, but the doctors and midwives miraculously saved them."

"Was that me?" asked Manya, tremulously. She had never been told about her birth and had no idea she'd been ill.

"Yes, Manya, you were that baby. You were both very poorly and had to stay in hospital for weeks. Your father sat by your mama's bedside almost every day. I went to the hospital too, but I was visiting you. You were a poor little thing; you were my little Myshka. Finally, when your mama was well enough to go home, she told your father she didn't want to take her baby because it was a girl. She was supposed to have a boy first."

Babushka looked at her granddaughter with tears in her eyes. She was reliving a nightmare that had been buried in the back of her memory for a long time. Manya couldn't speak. She discovered she was holding her breath and all she could manage was a small nod of her head. Her mother was insane. Why hadn't Babushka or her father told her before? All these years she had thought she had done some terrible thing which had made her mother so angry with her. A deep fury born of hurt and rejection began to well up in Manya and her eyes blazed.

But Babushka hadn't quite finished.

"Of course, your father brought you home, and he and I looked after you together. Eventually he had to explain to your mama that she would not be able to have any more children. Your mother broke down completely. It was as if her whole life had been ruined and she blamed you, her daughter. She only ever gave you one thing, Manya: your name. It means 'sea of bitterness'.

Chapter Seven

England - the present

On my way to school the next morning I thought about Jude and his gang and why they started picking on me. Big Ben and Tyrone were at my junior school. I've never been friends with them, but they used to be harmless. Big and a bit stupid, they would clump about together and the worst they would do would be to bump into someone on purpose and run off giggling together. But since Jude came to school last September, it's as if he's the leader they've been waiting for. Tyrone follows Jude and slobbery Big Ben follows Tyrone - usually with his mouth full of something and dribbling a lot of it down his front. They do whatever Jude tells them. To begin with they picked on the girls and the quiet people, but soon they started looking for something more challenging.

I've seen the gang target lots of boys in the class. They hide books, tip everything out of pencil cases, stuff homework down the toilet and try all sorts of annoying tricks. I've always tried to keep out of their way, but I suppose it had to be my turn at some point. I almost wish I'd got my turn over at the beginning. Their tactics have become meaner and dirtier, and I think they enjoyed spying on me yesterday. I could hear them laughing about how I nearly got run over.

"He would have made a mess on the road," smirked Jude.

"Like a big pile of strawberry jam," agreed Tyrone.

"Yeah, I'll have some," said Big Ben, only tuning in at the mention of food.

I wanted to make a comment about them being scared and running away from the figure in black, but I didn't know who it was. I think it might have been Louis. Louis is the firefighter who saved me and Gran from our house when it burnt down. It was Louis who asked Neelam if we could live at Autumn Days until my parents could be found. He comes to visit quite a lot and sometimes he takes me out. Once he took me to a pub to watch a Spurs match on their big screen, and sometimes we go to the park to play football if he's got time. I joke with him that he only comes to Autumn Days for the cake, but I know it's not really for that. He's always looking out for me and that's why I wonder if he was the mysterious figure. The only thing is, he wouldn't have run off if it had been him. He'd have pulled me out of the bush, and we would probably have had a bit of a laugh and he would've told me how to deal with the gang. I'm going to ask him next time he visits.

Apart from Jude we had one other new person who came into our class in September: Katie. I'd never really spoken to Katie, but today she arrived looking a bit worried and seemed to be making her way towards me. She'd just opened her mouth to speak, when Mrs Beaman came in and told us all to sit down, stop talking and get out our reading books. I couldn't imagine what Katie was going to say to me. It looked important.

I waited until break, thinking Katie might find me to say this important thing, but I didn't see her. I did see Jude.

"Today Billy," he said. "Today." He pointed his fingers at his eyes and then pointed them at me, threateningly. Big Ben and Tyrone tried to copy him, but Big Ben got it wrong and jabbed himself in the eye. I laughed and turned away so they wouldn't see.

At lunch I managed to get near the front of the queue and was first to sit down. I don't have a special friend, but I don't mind being by myself. It's easier that way because I don't like people questioning me. I don't want people asking about my parents because I don't know how to answer. I could say,

"Well I might have parents, but I don't know what happened to them."

It sounds a bit odd, so I could add,

"But it's okay because I live in an old people's

home and Neelam, one of the carers, has adopted me and Louis, my firefighter friend, visits a lot."

Too much information? Nobody at this school would understand.

Suddenly I found Katie sitting next to me.

"Just keep eating," she whispered dramatically. "And don't look at the queue."

I wouldn't have looked at the queue, but of course, when somebody tells you not to do something you can't help it. I looked at the queue. Jude, Big Ben and Tyrone were giggling together and furtively glancing in my direction.

"Listen," said Katie. "I was walking behind those pinheads this morning on my way to school and I heard what they were saying. I wanted to tell you this earlier, but I didn't get the chance."

"So what did they say?" I asked.

"They've got this really stupid idea that they're going to sit with you for lunch."

"That doesn't sound too bad!" I laughed, but I could feel a sort of panic rising. What did they have in mind today? They weren't going to sit with me to make friends, I was certain about that.

"Look," said Katie, "I'm just trying to help. I know about bullies and I can't stand it. I've seen what they're doing to you, and I'm offering to help."

I looked at Katie. Why would she want to help

me? What did she know about bullies? What had she seen them doing to me? All these questions were rushing into my brain, but I couldn't ask any of them because then she might ask *me* things. So I just nodded at her in what I hoped was an encouraging way.

"They have this gross idea. They're going to distract you and make you look away from your food, and while you're looking away, they're all going to spit on your plate. I'm telling you so you make sure you don't look away. Keep looking at your food at all times. Okay, they're coming, I'll stay here."

I felt a bit sick at the thought of three lots of spit on my plate, but I stayed where I was and kept eating.

"Ahh, that's lovely," said Jude. "Billy's got himself a girlfriend."

I felt my face changing colour. The wrong colour, and I looked down even further at my food as if I were studying the ingredients of my shepherd's pie.

Suddenly Jude pointed to the table behind me and shouted, "Look! Mrs Cannon's dyed her hair."

I was about to turn to look at Mrs Cannon's dyed hair when I felt Katie kick me. Just in time. Tyrone had already leaned forward, and his mouth was dangerously close to my plate.

"Her hair, it's bright orange!" persisted Jude.

36

Nothing from me. I kept my head firmly facing forward.

Then I felt a tap on my shoulder and I nearly turned round to see who it was but realised that, of course, it was Jude who had leaned around my back. I could smell him. I think he must brush his teeth with tuna toothpaste – that would account for his breath.

I kept my head down but lifted my eyes briefly to see what slobbery Big Ben and Tyrone were doing on the opposite side of the table. Big Ben's cheeks were bulging and there was dribble running down from one side of his mouth.

I could feel Katie shaking beside me. Was she scared? I looked at her, she was laughing! Jude angrily shoved the bench back and stood up.

"C'mon you two!" he snarled at Big Ben and Tyrone, "we don't want to sit with these two doughnuts, they're putting me off my food."

"Where are the doughnuts?" I heard Big Ben asking Jude.

And that was the beginning of my friendship with Katie.

Chapter Eight

Russia - sixteen years ago

Babushka died the day before the awards ceremony.

She never knew about the prize because the awards were only announced on the day of the presentation. She would have been so proud.

At Babushka's funeral, Manya had stolen a glance at her mother. Mrs Molchalin might have been sad at the death of her own mother, but if she was, she kept it well hidden. The expression on her blank face never changed. It made Manya feel angry until she considered her own features. Her eyes were not filled with tears, and her mouth was probably fixed in the same straight line she saw when she looked at herself in the mirror. She shook her head in alarm to think she might resemble her mother in any way.

Manya was devastated that Babushka had gone. Her grandmother had been the only person who had ever really loved her. Her father clearly appreciated her achievements, but Manya was aware that his pride was for her success, not for her. He had confirmed this in the tearoom after the ceremony when he seemed more concerned about impressing the other parents. He was delighted that Manya had been accepted at Pushkin but not for her sake. It was for him; he couldn't wait to show off.

Mr Molchalin took Manya to her new school soon after her fifteenth birthday. Her mother had neither celebrated the birthday, nor had she acknowledged the fact that Manya was going away to boarding school. Her father had acquired the new uniform and the books she needed. Manya had packed her belongings. She briefly considered how the Molchalin house would feel with just her parents in it, but only briefly. She was more concerned about how her own life would change.

When they arrived at school, Mr Molchalin helped Manya with her bags. An older girl showed them to Manya's room but immediately left them alone. They stood awkwardly for a moment, then Mr Molchalin put one hand on Manya's shoulder and said,
"I want you to do your very best here, Manya. You will make the name Molchalin great."
And without another word he left the room, shutting the door behind him.
Manya sat on the bed looking at the bags in a heap on the floor.
There was a knock on the door. It made her

jump and she stood up quickly. At the door stood
a boy with pale skin and very dark hair. He was
dressed in the Pushkin uniform of navy suit,
white shirt and bright red tie. Manya wondered
why he'd already changed into his uniform.
Lessons didn't begin until Monday.

"Hi, I'm Feliks. I'm in the room next door."

Manya waited for him to continue but after his
bold introduction he seemed to falter. She hadn't
thought about the other pupils at all. She hadn't
intended to get to know anybody. She had come
here to study. But here was this boy looking
eagerly at her, and she found herself speaking.

"I'm Manya. What are you good at?"

Feliks looked a little taken aback and Manya
realised she might have chosen her words a bit
more carefully.

"I s'pose I'm good at music," he said. "I think
that's how I got my place here. But I don't really
play an instrument, I compose. I use technology."

Technology - a word which appealed to Manya.

"What do you mean you use technology to
compose?"

"I'll show you if you like," said Feliks, and he
beckoned for her to follow him to his room next
door.

Feliks must have arrived a while ago because
he had already unpacked all his belongings. He
had an alarm clock on the table next to his bed,

folders on his desk and photos stuck on his wall.

"Is that your family?" she asked.

"Yes. I've got three sisters and a brother."

"Five children?" gaped Manya "Was your mum pleased to get rid of one?" She regretted her words when she saw Feliks' sorrowful expression.

"No," he said simply. "She cried a lot. She didn't want me to come here."

Manya needed to change the subject. The last thing she wanted to discuss was parents. Particularly mothers.

"So let's hear this music then," she said.

"I've just uploaded some of my pieces. Listen."

He clicked a few buttons on the laptop on his desk and a dark grey sea popped up. Quiet music was playing in the background which seemed to pulse in time with the waves. Manya was about to speak when the music changed tempo and became more dramatic, perfectly synchronised with the rhythm of the angry sea.

"I composed this last year," said Feliks. "I can't wait to use the computers here. They have these special programmes which can synchronise the sound and pictures more accurately.

"So what are you good at then?" he added.

Manya thought for a moment. For the first time in her life she considered her words. In the past she would have come back with a quick, "None of your business," but for some reason she

41

felt as though she could share something with Feliks.

"I'm not bad at maths, but I really love computer programming."

Suddenly a loud bell sounded in the corridor, followed by a voice shouting, "Dinner time. Everybody to the dining-room."

"Let's go," said Manya, looking at Feliks in his uniform and then at her own jeans and t-shirt. "But why don't you change out of your uniform. It'll be really embarrassing if you're the only one wearing it. I'll wait in my room."

"But I thought...." Manya didn't hear the rest, she had already shut the door.

Five minutes later, Manya and Feliks opened the massive oak door that led into the dining-room. Usually when pupils entered this vast room for the first time, they noticed the carved wooden panelling along the walls, the stained glass windows, the heavy, glass chandeliers or the large marble statue of Alexander Pushkin himself, Russia's greatest poet. But the only thing Manya and Felix noticed was the fact that all the other children were wearing their school uniforms.

One by one the other children stopped talking to each other and stared at them. A stern looking woman came over to them and, without bothering to spare them any humiliation, spoke in a voice that everyone else in the room could hear,

"When you are at Pushkin, you follow the rules. The rules state quite clearly that you are to wear school uniform in the dining-room. You are already late, so go and get your food.

Manya looked apologetically at Feliks. He had been right about wearing the uniform and now he would be angry with her.

This is why I don't want friends, she thought to herself miserably. *Something bad happens and then they don't like me anymore.*

They joined the queue to collect their plates of food. Manya was behind a very large girl with long bushy hair tied loosely in a ponytail which kept brushing across Manya's face. She would have liked to move out of the way, but she didn't dare turn round. Feliks was right behind her and would think she was getting him into even more trouble. As they approached the serving hatch, the large girl stepped backwards. The force of her immense weight pushed Manya off balance and she felt herself falling. She reached out to hold onto the only support available which unfortunately happened to be the girl's ponytail. As she felt the massive bulk fall on top of her, Manya wondered if this might be the end for her. It would be the shortest time any pupil had lasted at the famous school for the gifted and talented. Finding she had survived the ordeal, she desperately tried to push the girl off, but she was completely stuck. Lying, entwined on the floor with their arms and legs flailing, the pair had the appearance of some gigantic, upturned beetle.

The hall erupted into laughter. Somehow Manya managed to disentangle herself and she stood up. All she could see were pointing fingers and contorted faces. She didn't know whether to lash out or storm out. They were all laughing at her. All except Feliks.

"C'mon Manya, you need to see the funny side. It's worse for her," he said, pointing at the other girl who was still thrashing about on the floor.

Later that evening, as Manya got into her new bed in her new room at her new school, she reflected upon her first day. It wasn't exactly the start she would have liked, but she had done something very unexpected: she had made a friend.

Chapter Nine

England - the present

After school I asked Frank to help me with my maths homework. Frank lives on the Nostalgia floor at Autumn Days, but I'm not sure why because I don't think he has dementia. He can remember everything! He certainly remembers how to do maths. He doesn't do it the same way as we do maths at school, but he always helps me get the right answer.

I decided to tell him about Jude. I like telling Frank about school because it starts him off on one of his war stories. Nothing that happens to me could ever be as bad as the things that happened to Frank during the war. He was a soldier in the Second World War, and he likes telling me about the sergeant major who was always picking on him:

"I couldn't do anything right for that man. Me boots weren't shiny enough, me hair weren't short enough, me trousers weren't ironed enough. He told me I was so ugly me face weren't on straight enough! And all the time I would have to answer, 'Yes sir! No sir! Whatever you say sir!' Drove me crackers. He was in charge and I had to do everything he said.

"You see that's the answer son. When someone's in charge, you just need to go along with them."

But Jude isn't in charge," I pointed out.

"In that case just smack him one on the nose!" said Frank.

I laughed, but a serious voice behind me broke into our conversation. It was Mandy telling me not to get involved in any smacking.

"It's fine, Mandy, Frank was joking," I said.

Frank pulled a face and picked up his newspaper. He doesn't like Mandy.

Mandy had come over with a pile of little pancakes for me. She calls them blinis. She's always checking that I'm not in any trouble. Recently she's been going a bit over the top with it, almost as if she knows that Jude's gang has been making trouble for me.

Mandy's been the cook at Autumn Days forever. Well, as long as I can remember. I don't know why she wants to live here with all these old people because she's actually quite young. Even younger than Neelam, I think. She always looks out for me and it didn't surprise me that she'd been listening to the conversation about Jude.

I told Mandy I needed to do my homework, just to get away from her.

I went over to where Pascal was sitting, in his

46

usual chair by the entrance to Nostalgia. Pascal sits with his eyes shut a lot of the time and pretends to be asleep. But it's easy to tell when he's really asleep because his false teeth rattle when he breathes in. Pascal used to be a ballet dancer in Paris so he's very useful for French homework. I had a test coming up and I needed some help.

Pascal is another one who likes to listen to other people's conversations. As I sat down next to him, he opened his eyes and looked at me. When Pascal talks, his eyes flicker very quickly up and down, he stretches out all his fingers and twirls his hands around. It's as if all his movements are ballet poses. When he stands, he points his toes outwards. Neelam says he moves gracefully, but I think it's a bit weird.

"If I know anysing about bullies," said Pascal, in his French accent so it sounded like *boolies*, "dere's usually somesing going on in de background dat's making zem unhappy. And if somesing's going wrong at home, zey take it out on udder people. Dere was a boy called Etienne at my ballet school. He was good at everysing: arabesques, pliés and pirouettes, but he was mean to everyone. Once he took my shoes and put drawing pins in them! Many years later he told me his papa used to beat him wis a stick. I bet this boy Shude has a few problems of his own."

47

"Maybe," I said, realizing that he meant Jude, "but I wish he wouldn't take it out on me!"

"Well if I were you, I'd be kind to him and if you can't do zat, shust try to ignore him."

After my revision lesson with Pascal, I did quite well in the French test. Maybe a bit too well because I beat Jude and he couldn't wait to give me a hard time about it. He stomped down the corridor jeering, "Watch out everyone or you're gonna get knocked out by Billy's big head!"

"Yeah, big 'ead!" Big Ben shouted too, tripping over his feet and ending up face down in a pile of bags that had been left outside a classroom.

It was break time and Katie had gone to a choir rehearsal, so I walked over to a quiet area of the playing field where the gardening sheds are. I thought I might find an interesting pine cone or something to show Gran. It's always easier to talk to her if I have something to show her.

Suddenly I heard a footstep. Jude, Tyrone and Big Ben had crept up on me. I should have run away but I didn't want them to think I was frightened. Jude was strutting towards me when he spotted a big white bucket full of brown rainwater by the shed.

"Grab him!" he ordered his followers. They marched me over to the bucket. "Now let him have it," he yelled. "He doesn't have his mysterious friend to rescue him today!"

Tyrone and Big Ben plunged my head into the bucket. A few seconds later they pulled my head out and I took a big gulp of air. I could hear Jude laughing and then down went my head again. They kept pushing and pushing on my head in the water until I thought I would run out of breath. All I could think about was how, if I drowned in this bucket, I would never see Gran again and how sad she'd be. I don't know why I opened my eyes, but I did and all I could see was muddy water. I could hear the blood pounding in my head like a drum. I jerked my head sideways to try to tip up the bucket, but someone must have been holding it. I tried to wrench my hands free, but they were being gripped too tightly.

Then, suddenly, I felt them let go. I jerked my head out, took a huge gasp of air and fell onto my back in the mud. I couldn't open my eyes or hear anything, but I guessed Jude and his gang were running away before they got caught.

I just lay there wondering if I was dead, but I was happy to find I was still alive, and when I opened my eyes I could see the bucket lying on its side under the big conker tree. I would have liked to stay there a bit longer, but I had to go back into school. It was only eleven o'clock and there were still hours of lessons to get through. I walked as naturally as I could back into school and cautiously crept into the boys' changing rooms. Nobody was in there, so I went to a basin to splash water over my head to get rid of the mud from the bucket. A quick blast from the hand dryer made me appear, on the outside, almost normal. Inside I was wobbly. Jude's gang had nearly drowned me, and I didn't ever want to have to see them again. But I was going to have to face them in the next few minutes in history.

Mrs Cannon comes once a week specially to teach history to our class. She's one of the better teachers but she's old, and she's about to retire which is a pity because I quite like her lessons. Frank always complains that we don't do 'proper history' at school.

"The World Wars. That's the only history worth knowing about," he says. "And I know a thing or two about the World Wars."

Mrs Cannon arrived with a pile of books and a big smile.

"I have some very exciting news. I am going to give you the chance to enter my very final history competition!"

Some of the class groaned and Mrs Cannon looked a bit disappointed for a moment.

"I'm going to give you the chance to do a project about any period of history, from

50

anywhere in the world. Just think of the possibilities! You could go back as far as the Egyptians, or study space travel in the twentieth century. The choice is yours. I've brought some books for you to have a look through to help you with ideas. Are there any questions?"

Mrs Cannon's enthusiasm is catching and at least half the class put up their hands to ask questions like, "How long do we have?" and "What's the prize?" and Big Ben asked, "Can I do the history of food?"

I didn't listen to the answers. I was thinking about Frank's face when I ask him if he'll help me do a project on the Second World War.

Today had turned out quite well after all. I don't care about Jude, because *he's* a coward and *I'm* going to win the history project prize!

Chapter Ten

Russia - fifteen years ago

Manya had plenty to keep her busy. The work was more difficult than she was used to, and at first she struggled to keep up. She desperately wanted to get into the ICT suite but there never seemed to be any free time.

Mornings always began with school assembly where the Head would make an inspiring speech about how the Pushkin pupils were the elite, the best in the country. How, when they had completed their time at school, they would be expected to give something back to the Motherland. Manya didn't understand the speeches to begin with, but over time, the head teacher's words began to stick. Every day, as the children filed out of assembly, the Russian National Anthem would be played through the school's sound system. The pupils had to sing as they marched down the corridors to their classrooms. They were supposed to admire the displays on the walls which were covered with pictures of successful Russians and maps of glorious Russia.

Patriotism at Pushkin was extended to all areas of the curriculum. In history Manya learnt about victorious Russian battles; in geography she learnt about the vast extent of the country; and in music, science and language she was taught about brilliant musicians, daring cosmonauts and influential authors.

The teachers expected the best from all students at all times, and Manya found some of them intimidating. Mr Bykov taught General Studies and was particularly unpredictable.

One morning, the class was finishing the final chorus of the anthem as they entered the classroom. Mr Bykov, an enormous hulk of a man with a Rasputin beard, was waiting for them. Manya had learned early on not to talk in class unless invited to do so by the teacher so she stole a glance at Feliks and pursed her lips.

"Today we are going to learn to think outside the box," said Mr Bykov. "Do you know what that means?"

There was a pause as everyone tried to summon up the courage to answer. Feliks put up his hand, cautiously. "Is it when you have to think about things differently?" he asked, bravely.

"That's right, Feliks. I want you to start thinking creatively, unconventionally, from a new perspective.

Manya gave Feliks a friendly kick of encouragement under the desk. It felt good to

53

have an ally. For the first time since Sacha, Manya felt a connection with another person her own age. She gave him the slightest hint of a thumbs up.

"Let me give you an example," continued Mr Bykov. "What is two plus two?"

Mr Bykov waited while the children shifted uncomfortably in their seats.

"Come on! What is two plus two?"

Manya desperately wanted to answer but was too afraid. What if the answer wasn't four and Mr Bykov humiliated her? She kept her hands firmly under her knees.

A girl at the other side of the room tentatively put up her hand.

"Is it...erm...is it four?" she asked, timidly.

"Yes of course it's four!" snapped Mr Bykov. "But is two plus two always four?" he demanded.

"For example, what if you have two dogs plus two sausages? Then what do you have?"

There was silence. Most heads were down. Nobody wanted to be the one to answer.

"Nobody? Come on! Two dogs plus two sausages? Think outside the box!"

Silence

"The answer," said Mr Bykov, "is two dogs. Obviously. Think about what happened to the sausages."

The children didn't know whether to smile.

Manya just wished for the lesson to be over.

By the end of the first term Manya had decided that some of the classes were not worth attending. By the end of the first year she had discovered how to avoid one lesson altogether. Manya realised that if her name wasn't on the register, which was taken at the beginning of every lesson, she might not be missed. She decided the first lesson to give up should be Russian Language. She knew how to speak her own language, why did she need to study it? It helped that the language teacher was the oldest, longest serving member of staff. The little old man with thick glasses probably wouldn't even notice she was missing.

"Mr Popov," she ventured one morning in May, calling his name and putting up her hand at the same time, hoping not to be reprimanded for speaking out of turn. "Would it be possible to shut the blind? The sun is giving me a headache."

Mr Popov shuffled over to the blind and pulled at the string which had stuck. Manya knew it would stick because she had tied a couple of strategic knots in it before the lesson began. It gave her time to walk calmly to the teacher's desk and flick the computer screen to the page with the register. She didn't turn to look at the rest of the class but if she had, she would have seen every other child in the class staring at her, wide-eyed. Manya scrolled down to her name and deleted it. Manya Molchalin no longer existed in Mr Popov's class.

"Don't expect me in the language classes anymore," she had told Feliks later, when they had gone back to their rooms.

"Why?"

"I don't need to learn my own language. Just let me know if Mr Popov misses me."

Feliks had shrugged and gone back to his screen. It was one of the good things about him; he didn't ask too many questions.

At the start of her second year at Pushkin, Manya had a list of all the other classes she had decided to discontinue: art, music, design, religious studies and games. She had worked out that if she missed all these lessons it would give her an extra fourteen hours in the ICT suite. She had also worked out *how* to skip the lessons without being missed. It had taken a long time to hack into the school's attendance records but she wasn't going to tell anyone her secret. Not even Feliks.

Manya loved having a laptop in her room but the computers in the ICT suite were newer and much faster. Now she was able to sit, totally absorbed in front of a screen for hours at a time and she made sure she always sat in a corner. She discovered that if she kept her head down when anyone else came into the room, even if it was a whole class, nobody would question what she was doing there. They would assume she was working on something important, and that she had permission.

Feliks joined her as often as he could to work on his own projects, and he never asked Manya how she had managed to remove her name from the registers. One evening he knocked on her door.

"Manya, I don't want to know what you're up to because I don't want to get into trouble myself..."

"Why would you get into trouble?" asked Manya.

"I'd be an accessory to crime!" he replied.

"An accessory to crime? Excellent. What's that?"

"It means that if I know what you're doing and the teachers find out, I might be blamed for not telling them."

"It's no big deal. I just don't see the point in some subjects. I'm putting my time to better use."

"But what about the final exams? You have to pass all of them, or you won't get into university," said Feliks.

"Look," said Manya, "it's not your problem. I

am going to pass all the exams. Anyway, I don't know why you're worrying about me when you've got your music competition coming up."

"I just wish I knew what the other entries were going to be," said Feliks, "I haven't got a chance against Nikolai. He won last year, and he scored something like 89%."

Manya thought for a moment.

"Feliks, have you composed any funny music? Something totally ridiculous?"

"Yes, but I'm not entering with that," replied Feliks. "This is supposed to be serious. We have to compose music to go with a video of animals in springtime."

"Hmm, I wouldn't know where to start. But could you send me your funny music?" said Manya, "I just need to borrow it. Don't ask why or I might have to lock you up and throw away the key!"

Two days later Feliks was in Manya's room again. This time he hadn't knocked.

"How did you get Nikolai's piece of music?" he demanded angrily. "It's on my laptop. It came in an anonymous email with the subject, 'Your wish come true'. How did it get there?"

Manya looked at Feliks in astonishment,

"Why are you so angry? You told me you wished you knew what the other entries were.

58

Now you know Nikolai's."

"But that's cheating, Manya. What did you do? How did you get it? Did he see you in his room?"

"I didn't go to his room."

Feliks shook his head and stormed out.

Manya was confused. Feliks had said he wanted to know what the other entries were, and she had delivered. He was her friend and she had helped him. Isn't that what friends do? He must be a bit stressed about the competition, she thought. She would have liked to tell him not to worry; that he would certainly win the competition, but she didn't want to spoil the surprise...

Chapter Eleven

England - the present

After school, I raced back to Autumn Days to tell Frank about the history project, but he wasn't in his chair. I walked along the corridor towards his room. The door was shut but I could hear him shouting, "Take me home right now! Get me out of here. I don't live here! It's dangerous and I've had enough. Just take me home!"

When Frank was in the war, he had some really frightening experiences and sometimes he thinks he can hear guns or bombs.

I didn't stay to listen to anymore. I was disappointed because it could be hours or even days before Frank calms down. It must be horrible to remember frightening things and think they're real. I hoped he would be better soon because I was sure it would cheer him up to hear about the history project. I wanted to talk to Neelam about what had happened with Jude and the bucket, but she was too busy with Frank, so I went back to the lounge.

Mary was sitting in her chair and she lifted her hand in a sort of wave. She was wearing her red dress and it reminded me how she used to be before she had her stroke.

It was about a year ago when Mary first came to live at Autumn Days. She arrived looking all smart in her red dress and I thought she must be a visitor. She went around the lounge introducing herself to all the Oldies and shaking their hands. She sat down on one of the upright chairs, picked up a newspaper and started reading it. Every so often she would make a comment like, "Oh no, the dish ran away with the spoon!" or "Would you look at that, not even all the king's horses and all the king's men could put him back together again!" When I looked more closely, the newspaper was upside down!

It wasn't long before Mary had helped herself to a clipboard from Neelam's office. She started walking up and down the corridors making important notes on her clipboard. She would stop by a picture on the wall, shake her head and tut loudly. Then she'd write a note on her clipboard. Visitors would often mistake her for a member of staff and ask her the way to somebody's room, or how their relative was getting on. Mary would reply in her broad Irish accent, "Oh yes I know all about that. I sent him off to catch the bus for Dublin."

Neelam and I called her "The Convincer" because she could convince visitors that she was a visitor too. If she saw someone about to leave, she would grab her coat and follow them to the door. There's a special code on the door to make sure the Oldies don't leave by mistake and get lost. The visitor would press the code to open the door and Mary would say, "Would you mind holding the door for me?" Neelam would have to rush to the door and explain that Mary was a resident. Neelam was always very kind to Mary and would help her take off her coat and say, "Come on Mary, it's too windy to go out today, let's go back to the lounge and keep warm."

Mary became an expert convincer. One day Beryl's granddaughter had been visiting and let Mary through the door. Apparently, Mary managed to get right outside without anyone noticing, and she asked Beryl's granddaughter to get her a taxi. Luckily, she also asked the granddaughter why she had cut off the three blind mice's tails with a carving knife, so the granddaughter brought her back upstairs.

About six months ago Mary had a stroke. It meant she had to go to hospital in an ambulance and she stayed there for three weeks. I remember being very worried about her and Neelam was worried too. When Mary came back, I could hardly recognise her because something bad had happened to her face. It was as if half of it had melted. The right side of her mouth drooped down and so did her eye and her cheek. It gave me a bit of a shock to see her looking so different but when

I looked at the good side of her face, there was Mary with a smile and a special blink for me. Mary could still walk but she was hunched over, and when she tried to talk it was difficult to understand what she was saying. Neelam put her in a reclining chair next to Gran, and she slept most of the time to begin with. Gran didn't realize she was asleep and couldn't see that Mary's face was all lopsided so she just chatted away to her and didn't know that Mary wasn't saying anything back because Gran can't hear anyway. She'd talk in her funny language with words she'd made up,

"I've just been gardening gollyroots and you wouldn't believe how many blaberty frogs jumped out! There were too many folly fish fingers so they just scribbled up to me and I gave them a tiny poppet of silk..."

Mary is a bit better now, but she still can't talk very well. She has a string of shiny glass beads and she holds them in her hands running them through her fingers and muttering under her breath. Neelam says she's praying. She sometimes listens to me talking to Gran and nods her head, trying to join in the conversation, but I have to guess what she's saying.

I feel sad about Mary and I don't know how to help her. Neelam tells me to smile at her and say hello and that's enough. But I'd like to do more.

I sat down between Mary and Gran and told them what had happened at school with Jude and the bucket. Gran was smiling and nodding her head and every so often she'd say, "Oh that's nice dear," which I found a bit annoying because having your head shoved in a bucket isn't exactly nice! When I got to the bit about not being able to breathe, I felt a hand close softly around mine. It was Mary. I looked at her good eye and it was shining with tears. She blinked and I'm sure the look she gave me said, "Don't worry Billy, everything is going to be alright." I squeezed her hand back and said, "Thanks Mary, don't worry, I'll be fine."

Then Gran said, "Just put it all away in the box now." It was the most sensible thing she had ever said to me. I would put my worries in a box. I would be okay. I might not have parents, but I have all these kind, funny people looking out for me, wanting the best for me.

Chapter Twelve

Russia - fourteen years ago

Manya was hard at work early on the morning of Feliks's music competition. She had a few adjustments to make and then she wanted to spend some time with him to help calm his nerves.

"I think your entry is fabulous, Feliks," she said, "It was totally brilliant to use that video of the golden eagle chick. I love the bit where the chick's mum is trying to help, and she tips it over the edge of the nest. When it starts to fly the music's amazing!"

"Thanks, but don't you think the crescendo at the end is a bit too over-dramatic?" asked Feliks.

"No, it's perfect. Come on, let's go. I want to get a good seat."

The Great Hall was already filling up. This was the music technology students' most important event of the year and the other children were eager to see what had been created.

From her seat in the third row, Manya could quite easily see Feliks and the other competitors, all looking nervous. All except Nikolai who was clearly expecting to win. Feliks had refused to open the attachment in Manya's email which contained Nikolai's competition entry but Manya had watched it. After all, she had gone to the bother of obtaining it without Nikolai realising, and she was quite proud of herself. She acknowledged Nikolai's was an amazing piece of music accompanying the life cycle of a frog, from spawn to fully grown adult. She still thought Feliks would have had a good chance of winning without her assistance, but she wasn't taking any chances.

The Great Hall became silent as the first girl presented her work. A chestnut horse galloping through a field of spring flowers. It got plenty of applause, especially from the girls in the audience. The guest judge was very appreciative and gave a score of eighty-four. The bar was set high. The next three entries were rather mediocre in both quality and score. Manya lost interest and switched off, until suddenly it was Feliks's turn. The music and pictures were mesmerising. The audience erupted with applause at the eagle chick's flight. Manya watched Feliks's face change from a tight pained expression to a big smile of relief. It was over! The judge was very enthusiastic.

"Rarely have I heard such a precise and intricate piece of music from someone so young. An inspired choice of film, I congratulate you."

Feliks's score was added to the board: ninety-two per cent.

Manya could feel her heart beating nervously. She liked the feeling. So this was how it felt to be excited. She watched as Nikolai arrogantly stepped up to the stage and prepared the computer to show his entry. Manya was holding her breath as the music began.

Nikolai's self-satisfied expression turned to bewilderment as the fast-paced, catchy beat rose in volume. He turned to look at the screen. Three large frogs were jumping up and down on a wall and puffing out their cheeks as if in time to the comical melody. It was quite a sight. After a stunned silence, the children in the audience burst out laughing and clapping in time to the beat. Some were even stamping their feet. Red-faced, Nikolai rushed to stop the video, but it was too late. He desperately tried to find the correct file, but it was nowhere. Manya knew he wouldn't find it. She had deleted it and inserted the alternative frog video with the goofy music that Feliks had 'lent' her a few days earlier. She looked happily over to Feliks, expecting to see him looking jubilant in victory. His face was not that of a champion, it was livid. He looked at Manya, and his hostile expression felt like a sharp slap. Manya watched in dismay as he ran out of the hall.

"No, I'm not sorry," she insisted later.

"How could you do that to me?" Feliks said. "I thought you were my friend. I really wanted to win that competition and now I'll never know if I could have."

"But you did win."

"No, *you* cheated!" Feliks was shouting now. "Why did you do it? How did you do it? No, don't tell me. It's wrong, Manya. It's stealing. If this is what you've been working on all these months, you've been wasting your time. I don't think I can ever trust you again. How do I know you're not looking into all *my* private files, *my* emails, *all* my stuff?"

Manya didn't have time for Feliks's tantrums. She had helped him win the music prize, which was what he wanted, and he should be grateful. The skills she had discovered through her own investigation were skills she meant to use again. If she was able to hack into other computers without being discovered, she could find out lots of useful information. If she could change information even better. Right now she was in the process of changing her grades. She had worked out how to get into the main branch of the school system, and it was easy to give herself a grade 'A' from teachers who didn't even know who she was. There was no reason for them to know her as she never attended their lessons. She was

68

just surprised that nobody had noticed. Not one teacher had bothered to check why she was missing lessons; not one had questioned her constant presence in the ICT suite, and nobody had noticed she was changing her grades. The school's lack of computer safeguarding excited Manya. If she could crack the system at Pushkin, what else might she achieve?

She was disappointed that her friendship with Feliks had weakened but she had managed on her own before and she would manage again. They still sat together for meals, but they only discussed safe topics like maths homework or the quality of the food they were eating. Both of their passions were to do with technology, but Feliks didn't want to know about Manya's unauthorized activities, and Manya was disappointed at Feliks's absence of ambition and lack of recklessness.

Towards the end of the second and final year at Pushkin, both Manya and Feliks applied to Moscow State University. Universities set their own admissions tests, but it was a known fact that students from Pushkin were rarely rejected because they usually achieved such high grades. Manya wasn't going to achieve high grades unless she knew what the exam questions were going to be. It was one thing tampering with the school's system, but these exams were not going to be internally assessed, they would be sent to the central board. She needed to see the university exam papers and the answers too. She had done no revision, preferring to spend her time working out algorithms to enable her to hack into the complicated systems at the university. So far, she had found them impenetrable.

Then, just two days before the exams, Manya intercepted an email from the university to the head teacher explaining how to access the exam papers. There was not enough detail. She needed the password to open the files.

She spent all night in her room on her laptop. Even Manya wasn't daring enough to risk spending the night in the ICT suite. By morning she still hadn't found the code. Without the code she wouldn't find the University exam papers. Without the papers she had no chance of passing the exams. She would leave Pushkin with nothing.

In desperation Manya went for a walk to clear her head. She found herself at the entrance to the school and entered the huge double doors. The flat panel display screens were still showing different parts of the school. She felt a small twinge of guilt that she hadn't made the most of her time here. She hadn't used the gym, the music rooms or the library. She hadn't been a part of any team and she hadn't been made a prefect.

"Can I help you?" asked the lady behind the reception desk.

Manya saw the computer on the desk in front of the woman and made some quick calculations. Later she marvelled at her own ability to deceive, her speed of thought and her deviousness. How had this developed?

"Oh, yes please," she answered. "I made a birthday card for my mum and I need to print it. If I go and get my memory stick do you think you could print it for me?"

"I don't see why not. You go and get it and if I'm not busy I'll copy it for you."

"Thank you so much," beamed Manya, with what she hoped was a sweet smile.

It took less than five minutes for Manya to upload a Google Images card 'from daughter to mother' onto a new memory stick. She ran back to the entrance hall with the same nervous excitement she had felt during Feliks's music competition. The receptionist was on the phone, but she winked at Manya and motioned for her to sit down. It gave Manya time to see that the photocopier was in the room next door. If this was to work, she'd have to be quick. She wished she'd thought of something to print that would take a bit longer than a birthday card. Her heart had started pounding in her chest.

"Now where is that memory stick, dear," asked the receptionist. "I hope you know how to do this because I don't have a clue how these computers work," she giggled affectedly.

Manya went around to the other side of the large counter and looked at the screen in front of her. Her hand was trembling as she inserted the USB. Up flashed the hideous, pink birthday card.

"Oh, that is lovely!" squirmed the receptionist. "Your mum will be thrilled to bits when she receives this."

"Thank you," said Manya. "If you wouldn't mind going to the printer it will come out in a moment."

Manya's hand hovered over the *Print* key but as the receptionist bustled out of the room she had some other buttons to press first.

She opened the file icon at the bottom of the screen and up came all the documents. She didn't have time to find the exact file she was looking for, so she just clicked '*control all*' and then '*copy all*' to the USB and took a deep breath as the screen went blank for a moment.

In the middle of the screen the word '*loading*' came up, closely followed by '*copying docs...20%...30%*'

"Has it come through yet?" Manya called to the receptionist.

"I can't see it. Shall I come and help you?"

"No!" shouted Manya, a little too abruptly. "I mean, no thanks, it should arrive any second."

'75%.... 99%.... complete' the screen told Manya. She closed down the window, flicked back to the birthday card and pressed *Print* .

"Oh, here it comes," called the receptionist. "It looks fabulous!"

Manya almost forgot to wait for the woman to bring the card back out, she was in such a hurry to leave.

Back in her room four minutes later, Manya settled herself down to start her search. "*This could be a long process*," she thought, "*but the exam papers have to be in here somewhere...*"

Chapter Thirteen

England - the present

At half term Katie invited me to her house for the afternoon.

Katie's house is on a short road with a roundabout at the end. She has a little garden with apple trees and a compost heap. There aren't many flowers because Katie's mum says she doesn't want to worry about them getting damaged by a ball or a pretend galloping horse. I met Katie's twin sisters, Beth and Emily. They're only five and as soon as they saw me, they 'trotted' up to me and asked if I'd like to pat their ponies' noses. I didn't have a clue what they were talking about until Katie explained that they spend their whole time playing 'ponies', and I should feel honoured to be allowed to stroke the noses on my first visit. I felt a bit silly pretending to stroke thin air, but I must have done it properly because they both pulled at their imaginary reins and galloped off calling back to me, "We might let you ride them later!"

Katie and I played football, and the twins didn't seem to notice us at all until they needed me to be a farmer selling hay and Katie to be a bad dog-walker who hadn't shut the gate in the horse field. It was fun except when Beth got cross with me because I tried to stroke her pony the wrong way!

When we were having tea, Emily asked the question I'd been dreading:

"When's your mum coming to fetch you?"

"Neelam's coming to fetch me," I said, with a sinking feeling, knowing what was coming next.

"Who's Neelam?" she asked.

"Neelam looks after me," I said.

"Where's your mum?" asked Beth.

I didn't know how to answer.

"Where is she?" asked Emily.

It was an innocent question, but I was totally stumped. I could feel my face going red and I opened and shut my mouth like a fish, but I couldn't think of a word to say.

"I...um...er...well..."

Luckily Katie's mum came to my rescue. "Never mind that now, Emily. You finish your tea and then you can take your ponies for a quick ride before your bath."

Did Katie's mum suspect anything? I hadn't dealt with that situation very well. I suppose I should have been ready, but I wasn't. I don't want to lie, but I don't want anyone to know the truth either. I don't know any other child in the history of the world who has lived in an old people's home, and although I love living there and I love all the Oldies, I don't think anyone would understand. I would have to tell the whole story about the fire and about Gran and I'm not ready to do that. Not yet.

When Neelam came to fetch me, Katie's mum asked her to come in for a cup of tea.

"Say no! Please say no!" I silently pleaded.

"How kind," said Neelam, "just a quick one then."

And so, while Katie and I played angry farmers with Beth and Emily, Neelam told Katie's mum who she was and where I live.

"She's a very kind lady, Billy," said Neelam on the way home, "and she's promised not to tell anyone, not even Katie."

In an odd way I feel quite a relief that somebody outside the home knows my secret. I trust Katie's mum, and maybe it will be good to know she can help me out if Beth or Emily ask any more embarrassing questions.

I like being friends with Katie. She's fun and she plays football – what more could you ask for in a friend? There have been a few times when I've nearly invited her to Autumn Days, but I'm still not sure if it's a good idea. What if the Oldies say something rude to her? Beryl doesn't think anything of calling out to visitors, "You shouldn't wear that colour!" or "Are you a man because you look like a girl, go and get your hair cut!"

Once she told a new visitor to "go on a diet and have a good wash while you're about it."

What if she was rude to Katie?

What if Katie didn't understand dementia and laughed at Gran?

What if she asked *why* I live there?

What if she asked lots of questions about my parents?

So maybe not yet.

After half term, school got a bit better. Now that Katie and I go around together it's more difficult for Jude to get at me. I went to Katie's house again, and Neelam says I must ask her to come to Autumn Days.

When I was at Katie's for the second time, I noticed all the photos in her house. Photos of Katie with her mum and dad and her little sisters, photos of her grandparents, her aunts and uncles and one of her cousin's wedding last year. There are also pictures of Katie and her family on holiday.

Holidays look amazing. The sun shines all the time on holiday, and you spend your time in swimming pools, or on the beach or eating massive bowls of ice-cream. I've never been on a proper holiday, but I always go with the Oldies on their annual day trip to Southwold. I help push the wheelchairs past the bright beach huts which have funny names like Banana Patch and Jabba the Hut.

We all have an ice cream (except Beryl who doesn't like ice cream), and then I run down to the sea. The Oldies shout things like,

"Ooh be careful Billy; you're going to get your feet wet! Neelam, tell him to come back, there's a big wave coming!"

Or "Billy throw a stone in the sea for me!"

Or, in Gran's case, "Michael, don't put your fingers through the cage there's a good boy, it might bite!"

I stayed for tea. Katie's mum made sausage, chips and beans which is very different from the tea I usually have. Mandy normally makes some soup and then something a bit mushy. It's because a lot of the Oldies have lost their teeth and they can't chew properly. They have false teeth which don't work as well as real ones. I saw my Gran's teeth in a glass of water in our bathroom once. They were completely rank; all pink and white, smiling down at me from the shelf. I wrote a really good horror story in English the next day called, "Nightmare on the Bathroom Shelf". I didn't get a very good mark though. Mrs Beaman said it was "too far-fetched".

Frank was well enough to come out of his room and sit in his usual chair again today. Finally, I was able to tell him about the history project and his face lit up,

"Aw Billy, you've come to the right place. We'll make this the best blinkin' project the school has ever seen! Get yourself a pen and I'll start telling you some interesting facts about the war."

"I don't sink fighting is a nice sing to talk about," came Pascal's voice from the other side of the room. "I sink everybody shood luve one anoser,"

"Load of old tosh," said Frank. "Come with me, Billy,"

Frank has a box in his room full of books, diaries, letters and even his mum's ration books. He showed me his medals too, they were for bravery. There were some brilliant photos of Frank in his uniform. I could tell it was him – same crooked nose and slightly sticking out ears. They had funny haircuts back then and it made the men look much older than they really were. He told me he was twenty-one in one of the photos, but I thought he looked about fifty! I listened to Frank's stories and I wrote them down. Neelam let me use her laptop and I found some maps and timelines of events which I printed out. I started collecting all my bits of information and putting them in a file. I wondered why all schoolwork couldn't be as interesting as this.

A few days later we went to the Safety Centre. Year Seven always goes there. In the coach, Katie and I managed to sit a few rows behind Jude's gang so we could keep an eye on them. Jude and Tyrone were tearing their Safety Centre leaflets into little pieces and throwing them over Saira and Mina's heads. Big Ben was tearing crusts off a loaf of bread and throwing them into his mouth.

When we arrived, Katie and I were the last to jump down from the coach, and as we crossed the car park, I was surprised to see a fire-engine. Was Louis here? I wished I'd told him I was coming; it would be brilliant if I could introduce him to Katie and some of the others.

Mrs Beaman put us into groups and told us we were very lucky because the fire-brigade had come to help out, and the house fire presentation would be led by a real firefighter. I clenched my fists and hoped, *please let the firefighter be Louis!*

Jude, of course, was in my group but Katie wasn't. We were taken inside and shown how to throw a life ring if we saw someone in a lake, how to check our house for dangerous electrical equipment, and then someone in the group was invited to make a 999 call. We all wanted to be chosen, but Jude got picked. He was told to go into a phone box, pick up the receiver and press 999 on the keypad. He was supposed to say, "My name is Jude, I am at the corner of Palmar Avenue and Bassett Close and there is a fire at number seventy-two." A man in another room at the safety centre would pretend to be the emergency services and ask questions, but this is what happened:

Jude went into the phone box with a strange smirk on his face and dialled 999. He said, "Hi, my house is on fire. But don't rush 'cos it's only Grandma left inside, and she doesn't matter 'cos she's well old."

I suddenly felt very hot. As if I was standing on my head and all the blood had rushed into it. And inside my head I could see flames everywhere, and I could hear people shouting.

"Nobody here," shouted one voice.

"Quick in here, there's a kid!" shouted another.

I felt my legs collapse and I don't remember what happened next...

Chapter Fourteen

Russia - thirteen years ago

Manya was packing her suitcase when her father put his head round the door.

"Are you nearly ready to leave?" he asked.

"Papa, I'm nearly eighteen, I can manage a train journey by myself. It's too far for you to drive there and back in a day."

"I've got a business meeting in Moscow. I'm going anyway."

Manya didn't want her father to take her but she couldn't think of an excuse.

"I'd like to see the university anyway," he continued. "You know you're the first Molchalin to get into Moscow State."

"Yes I know, you keep telling me," said Manya. "and you can go out and tell all your friends too," she added nastily

Mr Molchalin didn't even notice the sarcasm. He couldn't wait to spread the news that his daughter had achieved straight 'A's to gain a place at Russia's most prestigious university.

Manya couldn't wait to leave. It was uncomfortable having Papa so proud of her exam results. And they were great results because she had got all the right answers. But she'd only got the right answers because she had cheated. She was proud of herself for being clever enough to crack the system and find model answers. It was just that little voice in the back of her head, "Manya, you are a cheat."

And she knew whose voice it was. Feliks's. He had got straight 'A's too but he had gained his through sheer hard work. Despite Feliks's judgement she was looking forward to seeing him almost as much as she was looking forward to not having to see her parents. Her mother had ignored her, as usual, right through the holidays and her father had been so tied up with his business, whatever that was, he hadn't had much time for Manya.

She had spent the past two months preparing for her Computer Science Course. Even though her entry into the university had been gained through unconventional means, she was determined to gain as much as she could from her three years of further education.

Feliks had no idea how Manya had passed all her exams, but he was generous enough to send her a message which said,

"Well done, see you there!"

In the car, Mr Molchalin appeared to be trying to make up for the fact that he hadn't had time for his daughter throughout the long summer holiday.

"Tell me all about this computer course," he had said as soon as he got in the car. And then, "Do you know anyone else going to Moscow State? Any good contacts?"

Manya had rolled her eyes at the question although her father couldn't see. *Why is it always about the contacts?* She asked herself.

"Will you have much leisure time?" Was another question.

"Are you going to get a job to earn extra money?

"Make sure you remain open-minded.

"Call me if you need any advice.

"Don't get involved with the wrong crowd."

On and on he went with the questions and the advice. Manya zoned out. *Why is he suddenly so interested in my well-being anyway?*

She did have one question for her father, "What time is your meeting, Papa?"

"Early afternoon. I'm afraid I won't be able to stay to help you find your way around."

"No problem, I'll be fine," Manya replied, rather too quickly.

Manya was glad that her father left almost immediately after arriving at the university. Her lodgings were on the opposite side of the campus from Feliks, but she didn't mind. She immediately set about finding where the best computers were kept and where the quickest internet was to be found. Friends had never been important to her and she declined every invitation to parties and social events during the first few weeks of term. Even when Feliks invited her to his eighteenth birthday party she replied,

"I don't know anyone – you'll have more fun without me."

One morning, they arranged to meet at one of the many coffee houses in Moscow.

"So Feliks, how's the music tech course going?" asked Manya.

"Fantastic," he replied. "We're looking at the influence of music in great Hollywood films."

Manya couldn't think of anything more boring.

"Wow! That must be interesting!" she said, trying not to sound sarcastic.

"It is. One day I'm going to win an Oscar for writing the music score for a great Russian film," he said. "But how's your computer science course? I hope you're not up to your old tricks again, hacking into people's private business."

"Of course not," lied Manya. "I'm making a lovely little game for small children with blue bunnies and pink butterflies."

"Manya I'm being serious. I'm the only person who knows what you can do, and you'd better keep it that way or you're going to get into a lot of trouble."

Manya found the work on her course disappointingly easy at first. She had already worked out for herself how to create games; she knew almost everything there was to know about files and data bases and she was almost insulted to be offered a module called, 'Introduction to Programming'.

So once again she found herself skipping lessons, or 'lectures' as they were now called. She didn't, however, intend to sit around doing nothing. Most of her time was spent working out how to gain access to illegal networks. She worked out how to read messages sent by the other students to each other. Then she found the personal details of some of the tutors. She sat for hours in the massive library, in corners where she wouldn't be disturbed.

A few weeks into term she noticed a new module that particularly caught her eye: 'computer security'.

"*Now this could be useful,*" she thought to herself.

Despite skipping some lectures, Manya made sure not to miss one word of the 'computer security' module. She was certain a time would come when a tutor would spark her interest with information she didn't already know about. And she was right because halfway through her first year she discovered how Russian cipher officers were considered the heroes and heroines of the Second World War. She would never forget the day when Professor Yenin, head of computer science, stood at the front of the huge lecture theatre and told the students about how, during World War II, the Germans were unable to decipher even one Soviet encrypted message. Manya would have loved being part of that team. Devising impenetrable codes which could be used to send messages during the war must have been the best job in the world!

"It was one of the most remarkable technological achievements in history and contributed to the eventual defeat of Germany," explained Professor Yenin.

"I've got a dream too," Manya told Feliks next time she met up with him. "One day a lecturer will tell his students that Manya Molchalin was responsible for one of the most remarkable technological achievements in history."

"And what will that be?" Feliks asked.

"I haven't worked that bit out yet," she replied, "but it could be something to do with code breaking."

Now Manya had a new goal, she spent many hours reading about encryption, code breaking and spies.

It was inevitable that Manya would be

inspired to do a little spying of her own. She started with Feliks. She learned that he would be going on a music tour of Austria with some of the students on his music course. She wasn't pleased to see he was communicating regularly with a girl called Karine and she was irritated to find that she cared. Manya was not a girl who usually experienced emotion of any kind, and jealousy was new to her. She turned her attention to something more appealing and one evening she found herself logging into a group of Third Year students who called themselves 'Goar V'. A quick search showed Manya that Goar Vartanyan was a Russian spy who uncovered a German plot to kill Winston Churchill and Franklin Roosevelt during World War II. What surprised Manya was that Goar was a woman.

Manya was able to intercept messages between members of the Goar V group which seemed to be activating a little spy ring of their own. Something to do with space technology. She couldn't follow exactly what they were up to but logging in at midnight every night became a habit. Within a few weeks she had found out the names of all the members of Goar V. They were all girls' names. Soon after that she found their photos. It became a sort of game for Manya to see if she could spot any of the group in the canteen, in the library or even in the sports halls. She worked out that the leader of the group was called Tatiana. Tatiana had short, bleached hair, always wore black, and spent much of her free time working with weights in the gym and perfecting her kick-boxing techniques with men twice her size.

One evening, just after midnight, Manya was in her room trying to connect to the Goar V group when there was a knock on the door. She couldn't remember when anyone had knocked on her door before and wondered who it could be. For a split second she hoped it might be Feliks, but then she remembered he was on his music tour with Karine.

"Who is it?" she called through the door.

No answer.

"Is somebody there?" she asked again, feeling anxious.

No answer.

Suddenly a confident low voice penetrated the silence. It was a voice Manya recognised only too well.

"Open the door, Manya."

Terrified, Manya opened the door to see a familiar figure standing in front of her...

Chapter Fifteen

England - the present

I awoke to find myself lying on the floor, on top of a big pile of coats. Mrs Beaman was sitting on a chair a bit too close to me, looking very worried.

"Billy," she said, "are you alright? The man leading your group said you fainted."

For a moment I couldn't think where I was. Then I saw Katie standing near Mrs Beaman and she was looking worried too.

"What happened?" she asked, "Saira told me your face went all red and your legs collapsed."

The Safety Centre! That's where I was. Jude had been making that phone call and he'd said something about letting his Gran go up in flames because she was old.

What had happened in my head? It was like a dream, but it wasn't a dream; it was more of a memory. Was I remembering the fire at my house from when I was three?

"I'm okay," I said. "Where's everyone else?"

The rest of the class were having lunch and Mrs Beaman said I could join them if I felt well enough. I noticed that Jude had been made to sit by himself at the far end of the room. I hoped he wouldn't be allowed to join in the afternoon activities because we still had to do the bit with the firefighter. Would it be Louis? I was about to ask Katie if she'd seen the firefighter and if she had, what did he look like, when Mrs Beaman told us to get back in our groups for our last activity. Jude had to stay in the lunch hall with one of the volunteers. We were led to the house that was supposed to be on fire, and there was the firefighter looking fantastic in his uniform...

It wasn't Louis.

The firefighter probably gave a good talk about what to do if there was a fire in your house and how to make sure you had a smoke alarm, but I wasn't really listening. I know about house fires. I know what firefighters do when they're on duty. Come to that I know what they do when they're off duty too because Louis tells me all about it.

We lined up at the end of our visit and thanked the volunteers. Jude was looking cross, but he'd managed to slip into the line near the front between Tyrone and Big Ben. Mrs Beaman opened the door and counted us out. As we were walking back across the car park to the coach, Big Ben gave Jude a push from behind. Jude turned round and tried to kick him, but Big Ben is, well he's pretty big, and he pushed forward. They both staggered sideways and fell. They fell towards the moving wheels of a second fire engine which had just appeared. Mrs Beaman screamed, the fire engine stopped immediately, and the door of the cab opened. Out jumped a firefighter who rushed towards Jude and Big Ben whose faces were completely white.

It was Louis!

"What do you think you're doing fooling around in a car park?" he said to Jude and Big Ben, angrily. "You've just come out of the Safety Centre! Didn't you listen to anything they told you in there? Do me a favour; next time you have to cross a road, make sure you hold tightly onto the hand of an adult!"

Jude and Big Ben's faces had changed from white to the colour of ketchup.

Mrs Beaman started to apologise, "I'm so sorry..." but Louis was already striding towards the building.

At that point he saw me and with a huge smile called out, "Billy mate, I didn't know you were here today, why didn't you tell me!"

I tried to stay cool, but it was really difficult.

"Hey Louis," I said as he came over to give me a high five.

"I'm coming round later. See you mate." And with that he was gone.

Everyone had gone quiet. Everyone was looking at me. Most of them had their mouths open and their eyes wide. Even Mrs Beaman.

"D…do you know him Billy?" she stuttered.

"Yeah, that's my mate Louis" I replied.

There was a hushed sort of awe as we got back into the bus. Jude had to sit next to Mrs Beaman, and Big Ben had to sit next to Miss Newton. That would ruin his plans to eat any food he still had in his bag. The rest of the class were looking at me with, I don't know what really, perhaps the word is respect.

Katie sat down next to me,

"Do you really know that firefighter? How do you know him? Why is he coming to visit you?"

"He's Louis, he's my friend and I'll tell you about him later…when nobody is listening!" I added in a loud voice for the benefit of Tyrone whose ear I could see pressed between the two seats in front.

Katie and I sat in silence. My insides were churning. Should I tell Katie where I live? Is now a good time?

I had the whole journey to think about it but by the time we got back to school I still hadn't made up my mind.

Katie and I walked out into the playground and I was about to leave when she grabbed my arm.

"Go on then, you said you'd tell me about the firefighter. Why don't I come to your house at the weekend and you can tell me all about him?"

I took a deep breath. "Look, Katie, I don't actually live in a house."

"Okay, your flat, your bungalow, the place where you live."

"I live in an old people's home." There, I'd said it. There was no going back.

There was silence while Katie digested my news.

After a very long pause Katie said, "That is so cool!"

Cool. She thought it was cool!

"Wow Billy why didn't you tell me before. What's it like?"

So I told Katie all about Autumn Days. About the long corridors, my room, the food, the garden and finally about the Oldies and Gran.

"It sounds mega brilliant! Please let me come. I really want to meet all these people and see your room and everything. Please Billy."

Katie didn't mind that I live in an old people's home. She hadn't laughed at me. She thought it was cool!

I was feeling really happy when I got home but I could hear Beryl's voice before I even got into the lounge.

"I tell you, somebody stole it!" she was yelling.

"It was on my dressing table and now it's gone!"

Neelam looked pleased to see me. I ran over and helped her lead Beryl to a chair.

"What's going on?" I asked.

"Beryl has lost a bracelet. She says it's been stolen, and she's accused just about everybody. Including me!"

Gran was sitting in a wheelchair. Her face was all pink and she looked very upset. I thought it would be a good idea to take her out of the room for a bit until things calmed down. The sun was shining, so I grabbed a couple of rugs and took her down in the lift and into the garden. I was pushing her around the flower beds when I saw one of my footballs on the grass, so I ran to pick it up. When I turned round, I saw that Gran was holding something. As I got closer my heart nearly jumped out of my body. She was holding a bracelet, running it round and round her fingers. I was pretty sure it wasn't hers.

"Gran, where did you find that bracelet?"

Gran looked at me as if she was trying to process what I'd just said.

"Well I think it was on the train," she said. "Yes, and she had a little dog on her knee."

She looked at me as if she had just got a complicated maths question right. I knew one thing for sure: Gran wasn't going to be able to tell me where she found that bracelet!

I pushed the wheelchair back to the lift wondering what to do. Could Gran really have stolen Beryl's bracelet? It just didn't make sense; Gran can hardly walk. And anyway, Gran would never steal anything.

Beryl was still shouting.

"I know it's you! Give it back!" This time she was pointing at Mary. Either Mary couldn't hear her, or she was ignoring Beryl. She just sat there with her own beads, gently nodding her head.

I went to get Gran a cup of tea thinking I was being clever. I hoped she would hand over the bracelet when I handed her the tea. It wasn't clever though. While I was pouring the tea, Gran was holding up the bracelet and Beryl saw it. She hobbled over to Gran and snatched it away.

"I should call the police, you thief!" she yelled.

Gran started crying, Beryl kept shouting and Neelam didn't know who to deal with first.

I wheeled Gran over to Frank and sat down between them.

Mandy appeared from the kitchen and walked over to Beryl. She grabbed both her arms and pulled her back to her chair where Beryl sat down heavily looking a bit surprised. Then Mandy told Beryl to calm down. She sounded quite angry.

Frank leaned towards me. "Blinking Rusky," he muttered, "I bet it was her who stole it."

I didn't really understand what he meant, but I guessed he was talking about Mandy. She's Russian.

Chapter Sixteen

Russia - twelve years ago

Manya looked at the figure standing in front of her. Tatiana.

She had been following Tatiana for so long, listening in to so many of the group conversations she felt she knew her, but realised she had never actually spoken to her before. She had never even seen her close up. Tatiana was smaller than Manya expected but with a steely, almost devouring expression that she hadn't noticed from a distance.

"Hello, Manya," said Tatiana.

How does she know my name? thought Manya. Her heart was beating, her mouth was dry.

"Hello. C...C...Come in," she managed.

Tatiana waited until Manya had shut the door behind them before she spoke again.

"Quite the little spy, aren't we?" she said, patronisingly.

"Look, I'm really sorry," said Manya. "I just stumbled on your group and I thought all the things you were talking about sounded really interesting."

"Don't even begin to think you can lie to me,

Manya. Ever," said Tatiana in a firm and steady voice. "I know you found us through a deliberate search. I know how long you've been tuning into our meetings; I know when you started following us and I know every time you came to watch me training."

Manya couldn't speak. *How did she know?* She had been so careful to keep a distance.

"In fact, Manya Molchalin, you will not have realised this, but we invited you to find us. One of our group had noticed your covert activities. She was impressed by how easily you were able to access so many of the University files and documents which are supposed to be secure. That *are* secure to everyone except the more advanced Black Hats."

"What is a Black Hat?" ventured Manya.

"A Black Hat is someone who breaks into computer networks with malicious intent. And that is what you do. You are showing great promise as a Black Hat." Tatiana smiled for the first time. Manya wasn't sure if the smile was friendly, so she didn't smile back.

"I'll stop following you, I promise," she faltered.

"No!" snapped Tatiana. "Don't you understand? The reason I am standing here right now is because you have been chosen."

"Chosen?"

"Yes. You have shown great skill in devising methods by which you are able to break into the secrets of computers. Your interest in Soviet encryption during the war shows your passion for learning. I am here to invite you to join Goar V."

Manya blinked. *How does she know about my essay on Soviet encryption?*

"What do I have to do?" she asked

"First, let me see your phone," said Tatiana, holding out her hand. Manya hesitated, but the look on Tatiana's face told her that refusal was not an option. She reached into her pocket and passed over her mobile.

"I like the way you have done your room, by the way," said Tatiana. "It must be a good view from that window when it's light."

Manya glanced over her shoulder. *The view? Why is she talking about the view?* She turned round again to see Tatiana examining her phone.

"Just as I thought, we'll have to upgrade you."

Manya felt a sudden wave of apprehension. "What if I don't want to join?" she said. "What if I'm quite happy on my own?"

"Believe me, Manya, you need us." said Tatiana. "I know about your mother and her secret obsessions. I know how you achieved straight 'A' grades to get your place here. We have been observing you for a long time. You would be very foolish to refuse. Not only because we are not accustomed to being refused but also because, by joining Goar V you will be opening yourself to opportunities you could not even begin to imagine."

"What do you mean?"

"We know you've been following our Space Tech programme with interest. Let's put it this way; we can use a student with your skills, and in return you will have access to information seen by very few people in Russia. At Pushkin you were encouraged, or should I say 'programmed' to love the Motherland. It was always assumed that you would give something back to the Motherland. Well I am giving you an opening; a chance to serve your country."

Tatiana walked towards the door.

"But wait!" pleaded Manya, "I don't know what you want me to do!"

"Nothing. You need to think about this carefully. I trust you won't need me to tell you how to contact me. But you might need this." And she threw Manya's phone onto her bed. "I have a good feeling about you, Manya, I don't think you're going to let me down."

Tatiana slipped out of the door and closed it silently behind her.

Manya stood for a moment trying to replay the scene. Had Tatiana, from the Goar V group, just offered her a place in the team? What was expected of her? What should she do?

She lay on her bed going over and over Tatiana's words. At some point she must have fallen asleep because it was light when she opened her eyes.

Should I ask Feliks? she wondered, sadly realising that he was the only person in the world who might listen to her and give her advice. Up until last night she had been totally focused, completely at ease with the path her life was following. Yes, she had mastered a useful skill in being able to access secret information, but it had always been on her terms, under her control. Tatiana made her nervous. If she joined Goar V she would be in a team. She had never been any good at group work at school. She simply didn't like other people. They always judged her and questioned her decisions. On the other hand, if she refused, Tatiana had implied something bad would happen. She resolved to find Feliks as soon as he got back from his music tour.

****

"What did you think I was going to say, Manya?" Feliks exclaimed a few days later. "You tell me that some weirdo from some freakish gang is threatening you and you're not sure what is the right thing to do! Honestly Manya, I know you've

102

always had an issue with knowing what's right and what's wrong, but this is a whole new level. You need to cut all contact with this Tatiana and get back to studying what you're here for. Forget about them, they're dangerous."

"But I haven't told you what the group is doing. She offered to..."

There was a quiet knock on the door, and it opened straight away. Feliks jumped up and walked towards Karine.

"Oh, sorry," said Karine, blushing, "I didn't know you were busy."

"It's fine," said Feliks, looking pointedly at Manya. "Manya was just leaving. You know what I think. Just forget about the whole thing, Manya." He put his hand on the open door as if encouraging her departure.

Manya slunk back across the university campus to her room. She was angry that Feliks had dismissed her so abruptly in favour of Karine. He didn't know anything. As she went to her desk and opened her laptop a message appeared.

Don't ever discuss our work with anyone again.

Chapter Seventeen

England - the present

By the time Beryl had her bracelet back on her wrist, everything had calmed down again. Mandy brought out the tea and cakes and I realised I was hungry. I hadn't managed to eat much lunch at the Safety Centre. I filled a plate with cakes and went to sit between Gran and Frank so I could tell them all about my trip. I was just about to speak when the door to Nostalgia opened and in walked Louis!

Everything went silent.

"Hi guys," he said in his usual greeting.

All the old ladies love Louis and I noticed them sitting up a little bit straighter. Some were patting their hair.

I stood up and Louis gave me the second high five of the day, then walked around the room stopping to chat with all the Oldies in turn. He wasn't wearing his firefighter's gear, but he still looked cool. He has to keep fit for his job and he goes to the gym a lot. The old ladies always talk about his muscles. It makes me feel a bit sick, so I went back to sit with Frank.

When Louis had finished talking to the Oldies, he went to get a big piece of cake from Mandy.

Finally he came to sit with me and Frank and I told him about Gran and the bracelet.

"I expect Beryl dropped it on a bush or something when she went outside and then your Gran must have picked it up," he suggested.

"That's what I thought," I replied. "But Neelam said Beryl hasn't been in the garden today, or at any time this week."

"It's a mystery," said Louis. "But how was the Safety Centre? I hope those two numbskulls aren't friends of yours. I hope I didn't embarrass you."

"Jude? A friend of mine? Not a chance! It was brilliant when you told them off – they went so red!"

"That's okay then, I just wanted to check with you. Listen Billy," said Louis as he finished his cake. "I can't stay but I'll come back soon, and we'll go and play football. Look after yourself."

As Louis left, Pascal came floating down the corridor from his bedroom twisting his hands and wailing in his French accent, "My golden toos-pick, it has gone! I know it was in my bathroom dis-morning because I remember I had a piece of toast stuck in my toos and I had to push it out with de toos-pick. And then I am putting it on de shelf."

Over the weekend, lots of other things started to go missing on the Nostalgia floor. After

Pascal's toothpick it was Mary's beads, then Neelam's silver hairclip and even Frank's gold watch. I secretly looked for all of it in Gran's room and it made me feel guilty. I didn't think she could have stolen anything, but I couldn't stop thinking about how she was the one who found Beryl's bracelet.

Things at school weren't going well either. On Monday morning I invited Katie to come to Autumn Days at the weekend which I was excited about, but she wasn't well on Wednesday and had to go home. She was off school on Thursday with some sickness bug and I knew Jude and his gang would see it as an opportunity to get at me.

At morning break I decided to head to the far corner of the playground so I could keep an eye on the gang. As I walked over, I felt someone kick me. I spun round expecting to see Jude, but it was Kieran from the year below. As he ran away giggling I felt another kick. This time it was Harry.

"Why did you kick me?" I shouted after him.

Then another kick and another. Surely Jude didn't have everyone on his side!

Mina came up to me and it felt like she was touching my back. I was about to lash out at her, but she calmly pulled something off my jacket and handed it to me. It was a sticky note with the words, *Kick me* in big black writing. Jude must have stuck it on as we crowded out of the classroom. I managed a small 'thanks', to Mina. She shrugged and walked away.

At lunchtime I offered Mr Brown, the caretaker, to help in the school garden digging up weeds because I thought Jude might not find me there. I was wrong. Mr Brown had forgotten his spade and went to fetch it from his shed. The gang appeared.

"Are you having fun with the two lips?" called Big Ben, pronouncing tulips as if he was being funny.

"He's going to forget-me-not!" snickered Jude

"Such a precious flower," sneered Tyrone.

"Yeah," said Jude, "face like a *cauli*flower!"

They ran off together. How long would they keep this up? I wished Katie would come back to school. I was certain she would laugh at Jude's stupid tricks.

When I got back to Autumn Days, I walked past Pascal and Frank who were both asleep and I went to Gran's chair. Beryl told me I should stop stomping like an elephant which didn't help my mood. I pulled up a chair next to Gran and started to tell her that I wasn't having a very good time at school. She had Dardar on her knee and was bouncing the doll up and down saying, "Dardar, Dardar, Dardar"

"Gran," I said. "Could you just try to listen to

me for a moment?"

"Michael, don't take that tone with me, you know I'm busy."

"I'm not Michael." I muttered through gritted teeth. "Sometimes I wish my mum and dad would come back and take me away from here,"

Neelam appeared behind me.

"Billy, what's the matter, this isn't like you."

I put my head in my hands and pulled at my hair. I hadn't wanted Neelam to hear that. It was all a bit too much: I couldn't seem to go anywhere without something bad happening.

I ran to my room, dived onto the bed and tried to think about watching a Spurs match, but it didn't work. All I could think about was how I didn't want to go to school tomorrow. I didn't want to have to face Jude and his horrible gang. I didn't know what they were going to do next.

Neelam came in and sat on the bed.

"Billy, I don't know what's happened, but I just want you to know how special you are to me. To all of us." she added softly. "You live here with me and all these old people and you never complain. You make us all so happy. Do you know how much we look forward to seeing you after school? It's like the sun coming out when you come home."

I could get through this. It's just a stupid gang.

Just ignore everything they do to me. Keep

out of their way.

On Friday I made it right through to lunch with nothing bad happening and I went outside for the last few minutes of break. One of the girls in my year came up to me and asked me to help her.

"My new pen fell down a hole over there, please could you help me get it out?"

I followed the girl to the edge of the playground where I saw the lid of a drainpipe had been removed.

"Down here?" I asked.

She nodded and ran off.

I put my hand down the drain, wondering where she had gone and heard a snapping sound. I suddenly felt a terrible pain shoot up my arm. I pulled out my hand and wrenched off the metal contraption that was clamped on one of my fingers. It was a mouse trap. I threw it down and looked over to where the girl was standing. She was with Jude who was handing her a Twix. Jude had bribed her! He had put the trap down the drain and told the girl she could have some chocolate if she asked me to help her find her non-existent pen.

I ran. I ran out of the playground and out of the school gates. I ran all the way back home. I saw an ambulance outside but didn't think anything of it. There were always ambulances

outside the home. I ran up the stairs. I wanted to
see familiar faces. I wanted to be with people who
were kind to me.

I burst into the lounge.

Gran's chair was empty...

Chapter Eighteen

Russia - eleven years ago

Manya had no choice. She was scared of Tatiana, and she had become too involved to back out now. What would the Goar V team do to her if she said, "Thanks team for letting me in on your secrets but I think I've had enough now."

She was actually rather proud to have been selected. They recognized her potential and she didn't want to let them down. After all, this was what she had been working up to her whole life. She allowed herself to dream about the possibilities of being part of a Russian spy ring. Something to do with space technology, Tatiana had said. Maybe one day the Motherland would uphold her, Manya Molchalin as a key figure in helping Russia to lead the Space Race.

Having made up her mind, Manya went to see if Tatiana was at the gym, but there was no sign of her, so she sat in a corner to wait. After three long hours she decided to go for a walk to stretch her legs. When she returned to her corner, she found a small envelope on the chair with the letters MM on the front. Manya Molchalin? Manya whipped her head round to see a small figure in black leggings disappearing through the door.

How did she know I was here? Manya wondered as she pocketed the paper and made her way to the library. She went to her usual desk and opened the paper, her fingers trembling.

There was a phone number and the words, "It's raining in Moscow and I forgot my umbrella."

That was all. What could this mean?

She rushed back to her room and dialled the number.

"Yes?" said a voice.

"It's raining in Moscow and I forgot my umbrella," breathed Manya.

"Keep your phone with you at all times," said the voice and the call was disconnected.

For a whole week Manya had trouble concentrating and every time she felt her phone vibrate it made her jump.

One afternoon, she was sitting in the library when the small figure appeared on a chair next to her, seemingly out of nowhere.

"Don't speak, just listen," whispered Tatiana. "We have decided to give you an opportunity to serve the Motherland, but you will need to make a few sacrifices. Firstly, you must not tell anyone where you are going or what you are doing, and that includes family."

That isn't going to be a problem, Manya thought to herself, but remained silent.

"You will stay here until we're ready for you, and then you will be called for your first mission."

"Will I complete my studies? Will I get my degree?" asked Manya.

"It all depends on timing. If you are committed, you will be ready at all times."

Tatiana made as if to leave but Manya grabbed her arm.

"Just tell me how you seem to know where I am all the time," she said.

Tatiana looked at her disdainfully. "I am surprised at you, Manya," she said. "For someone so devious you're not showing much intelligence." Think back to the day I came to your room and asked to see your phone. Do you remember when I commented on the view? You turned away from me for a split second. A big mistake. It gave me time to insert a tracker and a microphone. We have been monitoring you ever since. Use this as a lesson. Don't ever turn your back and don't trust anyone. Now you must destroy your current phone and take this one. Remember I promised you an upgrade?"

"I suppose this has an inbuilt tracker and microphone too? asked Manya.

Tatiana gave Manya another look of disdain and slipped away.

"I'll take that as a yes then," said Manya to herself.

To begin with, Manya felt special. Tatiana and her group had specifically chosen her, and she was accepted as part of a team that promised to achieve great things. She wasn't sure yet what was expected of her, but she would make sure she was ready for whatever they asked her to do.

After a few weeks she began to feel jittery. She knew the phone Tatiana had given her was keeping track of everywhere she went, everything she said, and everything she did. She began to feel self-conscious about speaking to anyone. She believed that every communication she made was being judged and analysed by the group. Sometimes she left her phone in her room just to get away from it, but she didn't dare stay away for too long in case they found out.

Manya had never been a sociable person and it hadn't really bothered her before, but suddenly she missed Feliks. Should she have taken his advice and backed off while she still had the chance?

Little by little Manya's anxiety grew. She spent long hours alone in her room, only venturing to the library when she was sure most people had left. But once she was in the library, she saw little point in studying. Tatiana might call her away on a mission at any time and then all her university work would go to waste and she wouldn't get her degree.

One afternoon she was walking towards the campus shop to buy some food. She had stopped going to the canteen, firstly because it was too busy with people she didn't know and secondly, she was worried about seeing people she did know. She had bought herself a cap with a large visor that she pulled down low so she wouldn't have to make eye contact with anyone. As she walked, she was aware of a group of students approaching. She kept her head firmly down.

"Manya?"

It was Feliks. Manya raised her head a little. What if Tatiana was listening? She wanted to talk to Feliks but not while she had her phone in her pocket.

"Manya?" he repeated. "Are you okay?"

She nodded but said nothing. Suddenly she felt annoyed with herself. *Why shouldn't I talk to Feliks?* She reached into her pocket and turned off the power on her phone.

"It's good to see you Feliks," she said. "How is the great composer? Have you written your masterpiece yet?"

It felt so easy to talk to Feliks. Normal. He told her about his work and asked how her studying was going.

"So I hope you've given up the spying idea," he

joked.

Manya suddenly felt very hot and she imagined a voice singing in her ear, *"I'm listening..."*

"Manya," continued Feliks, "please tell me you're not still involved with those..."

"Sorry Feliks," interrupted Manya, "I need to be...erm... somewhere."

She ran away from Feliks, back to her room and she turned on her phone again. Immediately a message flashed up on her screen.

"Do NOT turn off your phone when you are out. We know exactly where you are and who you are talking to. Be very careful."

Manya threw the phone onto the bed. She stood by the window and looked out, wondering how she could have let herself get into this situation. She looked at students walking past, laughing and chatting with their friends. They were so happy and so free. She wanted to be free too.

She began to think about her mother and how she had cut herself off from the world long ago. How had it started for her? Her mother was crazy, there was no doubt about it, but was she, Manya, heading the same way?

Over the next few weeks Manya felt herself spiralling down into a deeper and deeper depression and there was nothing she could do to stop it. Then, one night, she had a dream:

She dreamt she was back at home with Babushka. Babushka was teaching her how to bake a Russian honey cake and Manya was stirring the mixture. As she watched the gooey mess revolving around the bowl a tiny figure appeared at the edge, the figure continued to rotate but at the same time it grew bigger. It was Mrs Molchalin. Manya had dropped the spoon and stepped back but the mixture kept spinning. Her mother reached a hand towards Manya as if asking to be pulled out. Manya grasped her mother's arm, but Mrs Molchalin was pulling her back towards the bowl. Manya felt herself being dragged into the spiralling mixture...

She awoke with a jolt. *I am not heading the same way as her, I am not!* she told herself.

She quickly pulled on a pair of leggings and, even though it was still dark, she ran all the way to the lake at the far end of the campus. She hoped she wasn't making a mistake and paused for a few moments.

Come on, she urged herself, *I have to do this!*

Chapter Nineteen

England - the present

I looked at Gran's empty chair and tried to stay calm. I didn't usually come home at this time so maybe she was having her hair done or being taken for a little walk along the corridors. Maybe she was eating lunch?

Mandy was in the dining-room and asked why I was home so early.

"Where's Gran?" I shouted, trying not to sound panicked as I remembered the ambulance.

Mandy told me that Neelam had taken Gran to her room for a lie down. I ran to Gran's room. There were lots of people in the room wearing medical-looking uniforms. Neelam saw me and came out of the room shutting the door behind her.

"Billy, what are you doing here? I'm afraid your Gran wasn't feeling very well so I called the paramedics out to check up on her. I'm afraid she might have to go to hospital."

"It's because I was mean to her yesterday isn't it," I cried. "It's my fault!"

"Shh, Billy, of course it isn't your fault," said Neelam calmly, "I'm sure there's nothing to worry about."

But there was something to worry about because a few minutes later, Gran was wheeled out of her room on a stretcher and taken down in the lift.

I watched the ambulance leave Autumn Days from my window. What a terrible week. First the fire flashback at the Safety Centre, the jewellery going missing, Jude's horrible tricks and now Gran going to hospital. Neelam had been helping to make Gran comfortable in the ambulance and now she came straight up to my room.

"Billy, your Gran needs to go somewhere they can look after her properly. They can make her better in the hospital and then she can come home." She looked at me, I could tell she was worried.

****

Louis came back to visit again on Saturday afternoon. He was worried about Gran and about me being worried about Gran. He asked if I wanted to go out somewhere. It was quite sunny for February, so I asked him to take me to the park to play football. We sat on a bench for a while.

I wanted to ask Louis how he would deal with Jude and his gang and then I remembered about the mysterious figure in black who'd pulled me out of the road.

"Louis, have you got a black hoodie?"

Louis laughed, "Why do you want to know? Do you need to borrow one?"

"No," I said, "it's just that I thought I saw you a couple of weeks ago and you were in a black hoodie with the hood up."

"Not me," said Louis. "I've got a navy sweatshirt that I wear at the station sometimes, but I don't have any hoodies."

It wasn't Louis after all. Maybe I'll never find out who rescued me that day. I didn't want to tell Louis about being chased so I asked him about Gran instead.

"Do you think Gran is going to come home soon?"

"Billy, your Gran is very old and she's had a tough few years. We don't know if she lost her memory before the fire or if the fire caused her to forget everything, but despite what she's been through she's always cheerful. So many old people are grumpy and negative but she's lots of fun. That poor brain of hers is like a maze. She keeps losing her way and coming to a dead end. It's very confusing for her not being able to remember anything. Maybe she'll come back from hospital as right as rain, but whatever happens you know you'll always have me and Neelam."

"Do you think Gran might not come back?" I asked, afraid of what he might be saying.

"Come on Billy, we've got to be positive. It's no good worrying about things we have no control over. I expect Gran will be back at Autumn Days very soon, smiling and talking in that funny way of hers."

"But she's the only real family I've got. If she's not there, where will I go?" I asked, trying not to cry.

"Billy that's not true, we're *all* your family. Me, Neelam, Frank, Pascal, Beryl and even Mandy. I told you before, Neelam signed special papers which make her your guardian. She's responsible for you, just like a parent would be. After the fire, the authorities wanted to find a foster mum for you, someone who would take you to live in their house, but Neelam insisted you must stay with your Gran and promised to look after you until your parents came for you."

"But they haven't come for me have they," I said.

"Not yet, but nobody knows where they were that night so you mustn't give up hope. And in the meantime you'll just have to make do with me and Neelam. And I s'pose Neelam and I will have to put up with you," he added with a grin on his face.

He stood up and threw the football to me.

"Let's go back for tea.," he said. "I could eat a whole cake!"

****

Back at Autumn Days I asked Louis to tell me my fire story.

"But Billy, I've told you that story a hundred times, you must know it off by heart!

"But I like hearing it. It makes me believe there's still a chance that my parents are somewhere. Tell it from the bit when you arrived at the fire."

"Okay. So we'd been driving the fire truck pretty quickly down the lanes and we could see the glow of the fire from quite a distance in the darkness. Paul and I grabbed the hose and ran towards the house. The front door was locked so we had to smash it down.

"The hall was full of flames and the smoke was so thick we could hardly see. We were wearing oxygen masks and all the protective gear, and I was using our thermal imaging camera which shows if people are hidden by smoke or in darkness. We looked in the kitchen first, but nobody was in there and..."

"Don't forget the bit about the back door," I reminded him.

"That's right. I couldn't see much but I could see that the door was open, and the glass had been smashed."

"Do you think someone had tried to get out or had someone smashed the door to get in?"

"This is the big question. I haven't told you this before, but I think you're old enough to know now."

"Know what?" I asked, feeling excited. A new part of the story? Something I'd been too young to hear before?

"Well," continued Louis, "the police think somebody might have broken into your house just before the fire began."

"What? Why haven't you told me this before?" I asked.

"Billy, you were only three at the time. It's scary to think someone might have started the fire on purpose."

I couldn't believe what I was hearing. This was all new stuff he was telling me.

"So they don't think it was my parents running away from the fire?"

"Is that what you thought? Billy I'm so sorry, of course they didn't run away. *You* were in the house. No parent would run away, leaving their child in a burning house."

I felt a huge flood of relief. I'd always had this horrible thought that my parents had left me to burn, but of course, I'd never asked Louis. Probably because I didn't want it to be true.

"If someone broke into the house, could they have taken my parents? Kidnapped them I mean?"

"Billy mate, I'm really not sure I should be telling you all this. The police have been searching for your parents for nine years, but they still don't even have any names."

"Do you think they're still alive?"

"I think there's still hope, Billy." Louis paused for a moment before continuing with the story.

"Anyway, we made our way back through the hall to the lounge and I could see, through the thermal camera, the outline of a person. I could tell it was a small adult leaning forward and holding on to something, possibly the back of a chair. I tapped hard on Paul's shoulder and pointed in the direction of the person, the person who later turned out to be your Gran. We ran in, I picked her up and carried her through the flames in the hall and out into the fresh air. She was coughing badly but luckily didn't seem to be burnt. I heard the Watch Commander yelling into his radio, asking for more fire appliances.

"Paul and I left your Gran with the paramedics who had just arrived in an ambulance and ran back to the front door with the Watch Commander shouting after us, "Two minutes! I want you out in two minutes!"

We entered the house again and with our

124

backs to the wall, we edged our way up the stairs. The fire was spreading quickly, and we knew we had to be quick. We didn't find anybody in the first bedroom but then..."

"Go on Louis," I urged, you're just getting to the good bit!"

"...well then I saw you."

"Can you remember what you said?" I asked.

"What do you mean?"

"It's just that when we were at the Safety Centre, I think I had a flashback to the fire. It felt as if I was surrounded by flames and I heard someone shout, *there's a kid in here!*"

"You remember the flames?" asked Louis. "I might have said that, yes. Can you remember anything else?"

"Well I know you ran down the stairs with me because you've told me that before. But I think something happened after that."

"Yes, there was an explosion," said Louis. "After the fire was eventually put out, we found three gas cannisters in the kitchen. That's what caused the explosion."

I tried to grasp what he was saying. "Why would there be three gas cannisters?"

"Billy, this is a bit difficult to understand but it looked as though somebody wanted to make that explosion in your house. It's as if somebody started the fire on purpose."

"Do you mean somebody wanted to kill us? Kill my parents?"

"The police don't know. Obviously there's been a very long investigation but there were no signs that your parents were in the house at the time of the fire."

"So they *must* have been kidnapped," I said. "But how did you know about the fire? Did someone dial 999?"

"That's the other odd thing. Someone did report the fire and when we arrived there was this crazy-looking girl waving her arms about and yelling. When you and your Gran had left in the ambulance we went to find her, but she'd vanished. First I thought I'd imagined her, but Paul saw her too. It's a pity we didn't find her because she would've been an important witness. She might have seen if anybody had been lurking around the house before the fire started".

I was completely stunned by all this new stuff. I looked at Louis who seemed to be trying to decide whether to say something else.

"What is it, Louis?" I asked, "What aren't you telling me?"

Louis opened his mouth to speak when there was a cry from the kitchen. It sounded like, "Moya brosh!"

It was Mandy. She came running out of the kitchen and it looked as though she was clutching her heart. I jumped up.

"What's the matter Mandy? Are you okay?" I asked.

Mandy started rushing round the room, saying that her grandmother's brooch had gone missing. She went up to each of the oldies in turn and checked their hands as if she thought one of them might be holding it...

I felt a big wave of relief. It wasn't Gran who was taking the jewellery after all! She couldn't be the one if she was in hospital.

Frank stood up and came over to me and Louis.

"She's faking this," he muttered under his breath. "I reckon she's been stealing everything and now she's pretending something of hers has gone, just to avert suspicion. Seen it before in me army days."

Louis stood up,

"Billy I've really got to go."

"No!" I shouted, "You were just about to tell me something important, I know you were!"

Neelam came running into the lounge.

"What's going on? Why is everyone shouting?"

Louis bent down to pick up his wallet.

"Hang on a minute," he said. "Where are my keys?"

Chapter Twenty

Russia - ten years ago

Manya stood by the lake considering her options. If she carried this through, she risked being abandoned by Tatiana. All the skills she had mastered would be wasted.

"Think about how you will be able to help the Motherland!" Tatiana had said.

"One day you will make the name Molchalin great!" her father had said.

But what about her mother? *I am not going to end up like her,* she said to herself again, and dug her hand deep into her pocket. She pulled out her mobile, the one given to her by Tatiana. It was impossible to live like this, being watched all the time. It would drive her insane. She took her arm back and swung it forwards, letting go of the phone. She watched it loop in the air and fall into the black water. Rings appeared on the surface, circling wider and wider as if reproaching her, as if inviting her to dive in and retrieve the small machine that had caused her so much misery.

She waited until the last ripple had disappeared and then, with a whoop of joy she ran back up the hill in the direction of Feliks's room. She felt free.

Manya spent her final year at university enjoying herself. She spent time with Feliks and Karine. She even made some new friends who invited her to go out for meals with them, to concerts and the theatre. For the first time in Manya's life she felt happy. For a while she worried that Tatiana would come and find her, would be angry with her, but when nothing happened, she began to relax. She had no idea what to do with her life after she left university or whether Tatiana would come to find her after her graduation. Would there be consequences for not following Tatiana's rules? She tried not to think about it.

She left university with a second-class degree which didn't please her father, but she hardly cared about that.

"What next, Manya?" he had asked one day soon after she had returned home after her graduation.

"I have plans," she had lied and immediately left the room.

Her father did not look well. He had lost weight and had a greyness about him that made him look much older than his forty-eight years. Her mother, she assumed, was in her room, but it was clear she wasn't going to come out to see her daughter.

The truth was, Manya had no plans at all. She

started looking for jobs online but there was nothing that appealed to her. She thought something to do with computer programming might be interesting, but it didn't have quite the appeal of spying for her country. Every day she became more and more convinced that she had made a big mistake when she had thrown the phone in the lake.

One day, as she was scrolling through jobs on her laptop, a message came through:

"It's raining in Moscow and I forgot my umbrella."

Manya felt a thrill of excitement.

Another message came through almost immediately.

"The lake in Lopatinskiy Park at 16.00 today."

Manya could hardly wait for four o'clock to arrive. She kept going over and over in her head the reason for the meeting.

Is it possible Tatiana could still want me to work for her?

The more she thought about it the more she wanted it to be true. To spy for her country would be interesting, exciting, maybe even dangerous.

At three thirty, Manya set off for the park. She remembered what had happened last time she had stood by a lake and the closer she got to the park, the more apprehensive she became. *What if Tatiana is angry with me for losing contact?*

What if she has been waiting to punish me? She nearly turned around to go home but then she saw a small figure dressed in black, waiting on a bench overlooking the lake. Nervously, Manya sat next to her.

"Your first assignment," said Tatiana, handing over a package.

"What? An assignment? But I threw your phone in the lake!" exclaimed Manya in astonishment.

"You showed courage and individuality. You might have lost contact with us, but we never lost sight of you, Manya. Take this, read it and then destroy the evidence. I know you can do this."

And with that she was gone.

****

Two weeks later Manya was on board a flight heading for London, England. She had a small apartment waiting for her and when she arrived she found it completely ready, with the bed made up, a fridge full of food and a brand new computer sitting on a desk in the small living room.

Her assignment was to track down a scientist with the codename Galileo. The scientist was working on a project to create a telescope powerful enough to see into a black hole in space.

Manya had to begin by locating the scientist and then she had to work out what system was being used. It was supposed to be the easy part, but it took Manya more than two months to complete the task. It took a further six months before she was able to intercept messages. Sometimes, at the end of the day, Manya felt her head would spin completely off her body from concentrating so hard.

Tatiana didn't seem too concerned. In fact, she seemed to think Manya was making good progress and from time to time a gift would arrive at the apartment: a bowl of fruit, a new pair of trainers, a theatre ticket.

Manya didn't feel lonely and she liked living in England. She found the work interesting and absorbing, and she tried to take a walk in the nearby park at least once a day. A family with a little boy lived in the flat opposite and she sometimes stopped to smile at the child or nod to his mother.

"Isn't the blossom in the park beautiful?" the neighbour said to her one morning.

"Please," replied Manya because it was one of the few English words she knew. She hadn't understood a word her neighbour had said. The woman smiled and retreated into her flat.

One morning in early summer, Manya made a breakthrough. She found herself looking at a complicated diagram labelled with English words she didn't understand. She immediately copied it and sent it to the contact she had been given in Russia.

That evening an enormous wicker basket arrived from a shop she had never heard of, but the name 'Harrods' was plastered over every item inside. There was caviar from the Caspian Sea, oysters from Australia and white truffles from Northern Italy. The most expensive treats from around the world. Manya uncovered layer upon layer of delicacies, nibbling pistachio nuts and mixing them with Swiss chocolate from a box she found near the bottom of the basket. *Tatiana must be very pleased with me to send such an extravagant present,* she thought.

Manya had never seen anything like it. She stepped back from the basket and found herself laughing. She turned on some music and did a little dance all by herself. She stripped the blanket from her bed and set it on the floor for a picnic. As she happily crammed the expensive treats into her mouth, her only regret was that she didn't have anyone to share the feast with.

****

After a year of living in London, Manya still couldn't speak any English. She tried to shop in places where she would have to talk to somebody, but nobody ever seemed to have time for conversation and anyway, many of the people in

London didn't speak English either. She began to wish she hadn't deleted her name from the English lessons at school and bought herself a phrase book. She learnt three phrases:

"Thanks so much, I really appreciate it."

" Actually I'm running a bit behind,"

"Fancy a cuppa?"

When she couldn't find an occasion to use any of the phrases she gave up.

She had become so adept at infiltrating the files of 'Galileo' that she was certain Tatiana and her team in Russia must surely be able to create their own telescope by now. In England the telescope had the codename 'Episode Skyline', but Tatiana renamed it 'Mantel', short for 'Manya's Telescope'.

Tatiana was so pleased with Manya's progress she sent personal emails of congratulation:

"Keep up the good work. A few more months and you can come home. The Motherland will be proud of you."

Then, one morning, as Manya was settling herself at her desk to begin work, she noticed an encrypted message sent from Galileo to another scientist. She spent most of the morning trying to decipher the message and by lunchtime she was beginning to feel nervous. Did Galileo suspect something? As the sun was setting, Manya realised she hadn't eaten anything all day. She wasn't hungry. Her investigations had finally decoded the scientist's message:

"Urgent. Delete this address immediately and every file associated with it."

Her secret investigations had been intercepted and the British scientists had shut down their systems. She had lost contact completely. In desperation she grabbed her phone. Did she still have the tracker on Galileo's personal mobile? Manya managed to connect to the GPS and found she could trace the movements of the scientist. Yes! She was able to pinpoint the exact location, but what now? Should she tell Tatiana what had happened? Would Tatiana send help, or would she tell her to come straight back to Russia? Maybe it would be better to keep quiet. Manya had to make a decision.

Fearfully she dialled a number...

Chapter Twenty-one

England - the present

"Seriously, Neelam," said Louis. "I'm on a shift in an hour and I need my car keys."

I didn't know what to say. I'm sure we would have noticed someone taking Louis' keys. We only left them for a few moments when we went to get the cake.

"I'm going to have to look in the rooms Neelam. I won't move anything," said Louis, "I'll just have a quick check. Whoever is taking all this stuff is moving pretty quickly and that rules out most of the people here!"

I saw Neelam frown at Louis, but he did have a point. I know Frank thinks it's Mandy who's been taking all the jewellery and stuff, but I think he's got it wrong. I mean, Mandy is a bit odd, but I don't think she's a thief.

"Okay," Neelam sighed. "You and Billy have a quick look but don't touch anything."

It was quite exciting. Louis and I were private investigators searching for clues. First we decided to try all the rooms which had their doors open. We took it in turns to put our heads in to see if there was anything suspicious. After about ten rooms we could hear something that sounded a bit like singing. It was Beryl's voice coming from her room. Louis and I stood outside for a moment, listening.

"Come here little birdie," she was singing. "I've got you a present. Come here little birdie." There was a jangling sound.

We went into the room. Beryl was standing beside the open window leaning out. Louis rushed in. I think he thought she was going to fall out, but Beryl was so involved in what she was doing she didn't notice us. I watched as a big magpie flew down and perched on the windowsill. Beryl was jangling some keys in her hand: Louis' keys! She held them up to the magpie and the magpie took them in its beak.

"There you are, little birdie," sang Beryl. "I told you I would find you another present!" The magpie flew off with the keys. Louis was just too late to grab them, and he ran out of the room calling, "Don't let her fall out!"

"Beryl," I said to her, "have you made a friend?"

"Ooh yes, that's Birdie. He loves shiny things. I've given him all sorts of presents and he takes them to his nest over there in that tree. Have you got anything shiny?"

I looked out of the window to see Louis searching on the ground for his keys. I could see the magpie sitting on a branch with the keys in its beak. They must have been too heavy because the magpie suddenly dropped them. They fell down but only to the branch below and then they got stuck on a twig.

"You'll need a ladder," I called down to Louis.

"I haven't got time for that," he shouted back and started running towards the tree. He took a massive jump and held onto the branch with both hands. Then he sort of walked up the tree trunk, grabbed his keys and dropped down to the grass.

"Gotta go. See you mate," he shouted, and then he was gone.

I looked at Beryl who had been watching too.

"Blimey," she said. "What a dish!"

It turns out that Beryl had been taking all the watches, jewellery, Pascal's toothpick and Mandy's brooch, but she couldn't remember anything about it. When Gran found Beryl's bracelet in the garden, Beryl must have given it to the magpie who had dropped it onto the bush. Next time the gardener came, he put up a long ladder and found all the missing things near the magpie's nest. I thought it was really funny, but Beryl was a bit cross that Neelam had to keep checking up on her.

"Don't keep asking me if I've taken anything that's not mine. I would never do such a thing!" Beryl had forgotten all about it.

Despite the excitement with Beryl and the magpie I couldn't stop thinking about Gran in hospital and I kept asking Neelam if I could visit her. Finally she told me that Gran was well enough to see me. She had cooked some apple sauce for Gran because she said Gran was getting a bit thin. *What sort of place is this hospital if you starve while you're there?* I wondered.

The hospital was enormous and grey and miserable looking. There were lots of people looking ill and walking very slowly. There were visitors arriving with bunches of flowers but not many children. I could see why Neelam hadn't wanted me to come here, it was horrible.

She led me inside, up some stairs and along corridors. It smelt like a mixture of medicine, over-cooked food and disinfectant. It made me feel a bit ill myself. Once or twice people lying on beds on wheels were pushed past us. I hoped Gran didn't have to be pushed along corridors on her bed, I didn't think she would like that at all.

Eventually we came to a big room with lots of blue curtains hanging down from the ceiling. Some ladies smiled at me, but I struggled to smile back. All I could think of was that Gran shouldn't be in this place. The ladies looked very tired and their hair was all flat. The old ladies at Autumn Days have their hair done every week and they look quite smart. These ladies didn't look smart at all, just really old.

Neelam led me to a bed with one of the old ladies in it. "Look who I've brought to see you!" she said. The old lady opened one eye and then shut it again. Was that Gran? Surely not. Gran has bouncy hair, and she smiles and chats all the time. Gran has pink cheeks and bright eyes and colourful clothes. This lady looked grey and dull and floppy.

It *was* Gran.

Neelam chatted away, telling Gran all the news and how Frank has been helping me with my project. I noticed she didn't mention Beryl or the magpie. I sat on the chair next to the bed.

"Billy, don't you want to say hello to Gran?" she asked.

"What can I say?"

"How about you give her some apple?" And she got out the little bowl and a spoon. She showed me how to get a little bit of apple onto the spoon and slide it into Gran's mouth. Gran seemed to know that it was good for her and she chewed and swallowed but she still had her eyes shut. I had managed to get most of it in when she slowly opened her eyes, looked at me, and said in a croaky voice, "Ah Michael, there you are. You're a good boy."

"Hello Gran," I said, "I think you should try really hard to get better because we all miss you at Autumn Days and I don't think it's very nice here. And you need to get your hair done." That last bit slipped out by accident and I glanced at Neelam to see if she was cross, but she was smiling and nodding her head at me.

"Also, Gran, when I come home from school and I look at your empty chair it makes me really sad. Please come home. Please try to get better."

I reached into my rucksack and brought out Dardar. I handed her to Gran who carefully took the doll and gave it a gentle hug. Then she spoke to Dardar in a tiny voice that I could only just hear,

"I'm going to teach you how to skip later. I'm good at skipping."

Chapter Twenty-two

England - nine years ago

"They have severed connection." said Manya, breathlessly.

"What? How did this happen, did they suspect something? Were you careless?"

"No, Tatiana…"

"Don't use my name."

"Sorry. I don't know how it happened. I can try to reconnect."

"No. It's too late. If they have even the slightest idea that you have been stealing information from them, it could be a disaster. You need to come back to Russia. Now."

"But wait! I have a personal mobile connection," said Manya, desperate not to be cut off so abruptly.

"How is that going to help?"

"Well, I *think* I can trace the scientist's movements."

"*Thinking* at this stage is not an option," snapped Tatiana, impatiently.

"I can find Galileo," said Manya with a confidence she didn't feel.

"Okay. That might be useful. Stay where you are and await further instructions."

The line went dead. Manya tried to breathe more slowly. She had been close to panic when Tatiana told her to go back to Russia. She desperately wanted to finish her assignment.

She hadn't intended to tell Tatiana about the GPS tracker, but she had been left with no choice.

Manya's next instructions were not what she expected. She hoped she would to be told to lie low for a bit and then begin the whole process again of breaking into the cyber security systems. However, Tatiana's message had a sense of urgency:

Keep track of Galileo's whereabouts. Be prepared to follow.

Manya couldn't work out how she was supposed to follow Galileo, until the next morning when an envelope was pushed through her letterbox. Inside was a set of car keys. In the road outside Manya's flat was an old Ford Fiesta which hadn't been there before. Was she expected to drive all over the country looking for Galileo?

Leave now, read the next text message. She grabbed her jacket, shut the front door behind her and pressed the button on the car key. The orange lights on the Fiesta flashed twice. Manya hesitated. She wasn't at all sure about driving in England but had a feeling something important was going to happen. The GPS tracker showed that Galileo must have travelled some distance since yesterday and now appeared to have stopped in the middle of nowhere. She would have to drive towards the little blue dot on the map on her phone and hope the scientist was still there.

Every thirty minutes or so Manya pulled over to check the dot. It never moved. Had Galileo gone into hiding?

By late-afternoon Manya was still some distance from her target and was getting tired. She stopped at a service station to fill up the car and grabbed a coffee at the same time, needing to keep herself alert. Once back on the road she started trying to predict the outcome of this journey. Would she arrive to find Galileo setting up a new, secret laboratory to work in, or would she find an abandoned mobile phone in the middle of some cow field? There were no further instructions from Russia. Manya hoped they would contact her soon to tell her what to do next. It was pitch black by the time she finally reached her destination. The last part of her journey had been a long, winding lane which led to a small village. Everything was dark. No street lamps, nor any glimmer of life anywhere except from one of the houses, where a light was shining out of one of the downstairs rooms. Manya waited in the car for something to happen and, checking her phone again, discovered the house with the lights on was also the location of Galileo's phone. Was the scientist in there? She decided to get out and walk around the house. Maybe she would catch a glimpse of Galileo.

Suddenly two transit vans appeared in the lane. They were travelling slowly with their lights dimmed. The front doors of both vans opened, and two men sprang out from each. One of the men approached Manya. He was carrying lengths of thick rope in both his hands. This was not at all what she expected. Why had these men come and how had they known where to find Galileo? Then she remembered her own phone was also being tracked by the Russian team. How could she have been so stupid? She had led them straight to the person she now considered to be her own project. Galileo was *her* scientist!

"Where is it raining?" asked the man, gruffly, in Russian.

For a moment Manya was confused, but then she remembered the usual code.

"In Moscow and I forgot my umbrella," she answered. "Why are you here? What are you going to do?"

"Stay here," said the man, ignoring her question, "and follow us when we leave. Be ready."

It was too dark to see much but the other men had taken some heavy objects from the back of the van and were walking round to the back of the house.

It was completely silent for a few minutes. Manya regretted telling Tatiana she had located Galileo. The whole program had gone way too far out of control. What were the men going to do to the scientist?

There was a tremendous crash. It was the sound of breaking glass followed by a scream. Manya ran round to the back of the house where she could see, through a widow, leaping flames climbing the walls of a room. The four men were bundling two people out of the house. A man and a woman. Both had been tied up, their hands pinned to their sides, with the rope. They were both shouting but the only words Manya could make out were, "My baby!"

"No!" shouted Manya in Russian to the men, "there's a baby in the house!"

The men ignored Manya and dragged the two desperate, writhing figures to the back of the vans. One in each. Manya ran after them and then looked back to the house. The flames were clearly visible from the road.

"Pozar!" she screamed, because she didn't know the English word for fire, "Pozar!"

As the men ran round to the front of the vans, one of them approached Manya and slapped her hard across the face. Stunned, she jumped backwards in pain and watched as the man leapt into the driver's seat and sped away with the other van following closely behind.

Manya ran back to the house, sobbing. A baby was inside the burning house and she had to get in to save it. The broken kitchen door was hanging off its hinges, but she couldn't get through it because of the flames which, by now were now licking the ceiling. She ran to the front of the house and tried the door. It was locked. She looked about for something to throw at a window. If she could break the glass, she might be able to climb in and reach the child before the fire did. She gathered up a fistful of pebbles and flung them at the window, but they just bounced off. She ran out to the lane, desperately searching for something heavy enough to break the glass.

The fire was spreading throughout the ground floor of the house and just as Manya began to give up hope, she heard a vehicle driving at speed, and soon headlights appeared. A fire engine. One of the neighbours must have called it. Manya ran towards it, waving her arms and shouting for the firefighters to hurry.

"Baybee!" she yelled, hoping she had the correct word, and pointing to the house.

The firefighters lost no time. Two of them smashed down the front door and disappeared into the burning house. A few moments later they

147

reappeared, carrying what seemed to be an elderly lady. An ambulance had arrived, and the lady was gently lifted in by the paramedics. The firefighters ran back into the house and, after what seemed to Manya an eternity, one of them emerged from the burning house carrying a small boy wearing pyjamas. Manya was sitting by the edge of the road, rocking backwards and forwards.

"What have I done? I didn't know!" she cried silently to herself. "I didn't know Galileo had a family. A child!"

She watched as the firefighter carried the little boy towards the ambulance. The child's head was looking backwards over the man's shoulder and he was staring with round, frightened eyes towards the place where Manya was sitting. Their eyes met for a moment.

A massive explosion jerked Manya back into consciousness. The house seemed to be ripping itself to pieces before her very eyes. The wailing noise of a siren was getting louder and Manya realised she needed to get away. This was her fault, and the police were coming. She rushed to her car and drove over the hill, out of the village just before the police arrived...

Chapter Twenty-three

England - the present

I hoped my visit with Gran might have helped her in some way, but it was sad when we got back from the hospital and her chair was still empty. Neelam said Gran had a long way to go before she was well enough to come home. Frank was in a good mood though, so we worked on my project which was due in the next day. I was really pleased with it. It probably wasn't as neat as it could have been, but I'd drawn lots of pictures to go with the writing and Frank had let me print out some of his photos. I really wanted to win the project prize but there were lots of clever people in my year, so I probably didn't stand a chance. At the back of the project on the last page I stuck in the picture of Frank in his uniform and below it I wrote, "With special thanks to my good friend Frank who lived through the war and told me all about his experiences." I thought it sounded very professional and a bit like the sort of thing you might read in a real book.

On Monday I handed in my project. I was quite optimistic when I saw the first few scruffy folders and files that had already been handed in. But it soon became clear, I didn't stand a chance against the beautiful book Mina brought in. It was all bound and covered with plastic. Her project was about Egypt and she'd even made a pyramid out of Lego bricks. Still, I'd enjoyed writing about the war and Frank had taught me so much that winning the prize didn't matter. Not really. Well, actually it did matter because I'd never tried so hard with anything before in my life!

Mrs Cannon collected all the projects and told us it might take her some time to read them all, but she would try to give us the results on Friday. For the rest of the week I tried to be friendly to everyone to get some good karma and I even tried to smile at Jude, but that was going a bit too far, especially as he looked at me and said, "Why are you showing me your teeth? Don't they fit in your mouth anymore?"

Friday came and I felt nervous. I knew deep down that I wasn't going to win but I couldn't help hoping. Mrs Cannon came into the classroom and announced, "Today is the day I am going to reveal the winner of my final history project prize!"

I looked at Mina to see how she would react when her name was called out.

I vaguely heard Mrs Cannon say, "I was delighted with your work. It seems you have all found a period in history that interests you.

However, there was one project that stood out as a project of passion. The stories, the facts, the incredible detail and the pictures all made me feel as though I was actually there, living during those terrible times. The winner is... Billy for his astounding project on the Second World War!"

Billy? Me? I had won?

I had won!

The class started clapping and Katie was cheering, and I just stood there like an idiot. I had won the history prize. I couldn't wait to tell Frank.

After school I ran all the way home and burst through the door into the Nostalgia lounge.

"Frank we won! We won the history prize!" He was up and out of his chair and he took me by the hands, and we did a lap of honour around the lounge. The other Oldies were clapping, and Beryl kept repeating, "If it's a party, mine's a brandy!"

I was about to go to tell Mary about the project when Neelam beckoned me and I followed her towards my room. Outside my door I noticed that Gran's door, which had been shut for over a week, was open. Somebody was in there. My heart felt like it was going to jump out of my chest as I saw a man in a black suit sitting on the end of the bed. It was the doctor. I rushed in and there was Gran sitting up in bed wearing her blue nightdress and her face looking all pink.

"Michael!" she called, "I'm so pleased you're back. Run along and eat your tea while I go and have my hair done, I'm going to the theatre tonight."

Gran was home!

****

Now that Gran was back home, I could invite Katie. On Saturday morning I gave her the "Grand Tour" of Autumn Days and introduced her to all my friends. Frank was in great form and told us a funny story about one of the soldiers in his squad.

"We was all lined up with our uniforms lookin' spick 'n' span. Our hair all tidy, our nails clean and our boots shiny. One poor bloke, Pete his name was, well he hadn't polished his boots enough. There was this tiny speck o'dust on his right foot. That old sergeant went ballistic! Shouted and spat somethin' terrible. He told Pete he wasn't good enough and even though it was his afternoon off he was going to get punished. D'you know what he had to do? It was a beautiful afternoon, but Pete was made to climb up onto the roof of our shed with a broom to sweep all the sunshine off it! All the sunshine! How was he supposed to sweep sunshine off a shed? There wasn't a cloud in the sky and there he was brushin' and brushin'! Couldn't come down till eight o' clock when the sun set. You can bet Pete had the shiniest boots in the whole platoon after that! He never wanted to brush sunshine again!"

Katie said Frank's story was hilarious and of course, Frank loved that. He stood up and did a little dance around his chair which made Katie laugh even more. And because we were both in a silly mood after that it didn't matter when Beryl called out to us, "Why did they let these two young hooligans in? They should be arrested for looking like that. Rips in their jeans, writing on their shirts, it's indecent!".

Katie didn't flinch at all when she saw Mary, and she had a chat with Gran. This is what they both said.

Katie: Hello, I'm Billy's friend Katie.

Gran: Oh I'm very pleased to meet you but who is Billy?

Katie: Billy's your grandson, look he's here, next to me.

Gran: No, you are very much mistaken, that's my *son,* Michael.

"My son Michael," she said! Gran has often called me Michael, but she's never actually said "my son" before. After Katie had gone, I went to ask Gran about her son Michael because I thought she might be getting her memory back. She might be able to remember where my parents

153

were on the night of the fire. If Gran remembers,
I might get my parents back!

Chapter Twenty-four

Russia - nine years ago

Manya sat on a bench in Lopatinskiy Park reflecting on all that had happened to her since she last sat on this same bench. It was almost a year ago that she had nervously listened to her instructions from Tatiana. She should have run away. She should never have got involved. How she wished she could go back to that day and change it.

Here she was with no home, no family, no friends, no money and no job. But worst of all was the memory of the little boy being carried away from his burning house. Last week the little boy had parents who loved him and now, because of her, they were gone. Where were they now? Were they even alive?

Manya shivered and pulled her coat tightly around herself.

She thought about her own parents. Would she have been better off if they had been taken away from her when she was little? Were they to blame for creating the monster she had become? She would never find out now. She would never see either of them again.

After driving away from the burning house,

Manya had found the nearest international airport and boarded the first available flight to Moscow. She had taken the train to Smolensk and a taxi to her home. Her father would surely be happy to see her? She might not have contacted him since leaving for England, but she was still his daughter and he had always been proud of her achievements.

She stood on the doorstep and wished she had tried to make herself look a bit more presentable. Her hair was unbrushed and she hadn't slept properly for two days. There was a big bruise on her cheek from where the Russian had slapped her. She took a deep breath and rang the doorbell. There was no sound of movement inside the house. She rang again. And again. The sound of slow, heavy footsteps could be heard approaching the door. Had her father's health deteriorated this much?

The door opened slowly but it wasn't her father. It was Mrs Molchalin.

Manya didn't know how to address this stranger who had never acknowledged her existence.

"Where is Papa? Is he okay?"

Mrs Molchalin's eyes looked straight past Manya as if she couldn't see her own, dishevelled daughter on the doorstep.

"Mr Molchalin died three months ago," she

said, shutting the door again.

Manya felt the final piece of her world come crashing in on her. She turned around and sat on the doorstep. Her father had died, and she hadn't even known.

Filled with guilt, Manya wandered to the cemetery where Baboushka had been buried, expecting to find her father's grave nearby. There were a few new plaques but nothing with the name Dimitri Molchalin on.

Poor Papa, thought Manya, *he hasn't had a proper burial.* She wondered if her mother had even arranged a funeral. She knew very little about her father. He had always been more interested in pushing his daughter towards a goal she didn't quite understand. He had never spoken about his own parents or any family. Manya knew he had been an engineer of some sort, but he had never spoken about his work. A horrible realisation crept up on her that she had not been a good daughter. He had wanted the best for her and even though he went about it in a strange way, he meant well. All she had done in return was to avoid him, ignore him and, lately, abandon him.

Now, sitting on the bench in the park, she knew she must pull herself together, and a sense of self-preservation kicked in. She needed to make a plan. It was too late for her to do anything for her father, but she could try to ease her mind about the terrible thing she had done to the little English boy. And she wanted to remain part of the Russian team. She didn't like some of the methods they used, but she still wanted to be involved.

She stood up and began to walk around the lake. Round and round thinking, thinking. After ten laps of the lake she had the beginnings of a plan. It could work, but only if the boy's parents were still alive. She still had the phone Tatiana had given her and she sent a message.

It's raining in the park in Smolensk and I don't have an umbrella.

It was worth a try.

Manya waited a long time She dared not leave the park in case Tatiana should come when she was away.

Eventually the familiar figure in black appeared on Manya's bench. During the time she was waiting, Manya had worked out the details of her plan and she described it to Tatiana.

Tatiana listened. She nodded her head once or twice and when Manya had finished she was silent for a few minutes.

"I wasn't aware of a child but yes, Manya, I think it could be helpful. Take a few days to clean yourself up and I will make the arrangements.

Once the child has been located and we have secured a position for you, I will make contact."

And so it was, that a few weeks later, a refreshed, clean and hopeful young lady with a strong Russian accent boarded a plane for England. She was very happy to change her name. No more 'Sea of Bitterness', it would be Mandy from now on. Her destination was an old people's home not too far from the house which had burned down just over two months earlier. She had been given a job as a cleaner, but this would not be her only income. Her bank account would be receiving secret transfers on the condition that she sent at least one photo of a particular little boy every month to a secure email address. She assumed Tatiana knew where Galileo was being held and the photo was being used to blackmail the scientist. She could imagine Tatiana showing the photo to Galileo:

"Here is the latest photo of your little boy. He is safe and well, and one of our people is in close contact with him. If you want your little boy to stay safe and well, you will do exactly what I tell you."

Galileo would have no choice but to work for the Russian team.

Manya felt proud that with her assistance, the Motherland was still able to progress with the space project. At the same time, she was satisfied that the child was being taken care of.

Mandy didn't like cleaning and she wasn't very good at it. She struggled with the language and had to remember her new name. She had to report to Neelam who ran the home and, after a few weeks she felt confident enough to ask Neelam some questions.

She asked why the little boy was living in a home for old people.

"You mean Billy, that's the name we gave him. It's a very sad story, Mandy. About two months ago there was a terrible fire at a house in a small village not far from here," Neelam explained. "The fire completely destroyed the house. The firefighters managed to rescue Billy and his Gran, but they couldn't find anybody else."

Mandy asked if there were any relatives who could look after them.

"There might be," said Neelam, "But there was nothing left in the house, so we have no idea who these people are. No papers, no documents, not even any photos. Gran has no memory and Billy hasn't spoken at all yet. I'm just hoping they'll remember something soon.

Neelam continued, "The neighbours told the police that the family had only arrived that day, the day of the fire. The police have spent the last few weeks trying to track down Billy's parents. They've been keeping me up to date, but the only thing they've discovered so far is through the agents who let the house. It turns out that the family were using false names. They must have been running away from someone."

Mandy knew exactly who they had been running away from but said nothing.

"Louis, one of the firefighters who rescued Billy and Gran, is a good friend of mine," said Neelam. "He was worried about them and asked if there was any room here at Autumn Days. I had space and I couldn't bear to see Billy separated from his Gran, so I agreed to let them live here until we find Billy's parents."

Mandy wanted to know what would happen if Billy's parents were never found.

"I just hope we *do* find them." replied Neelam.

****

For three years Mandy cleaned the rooms at Autumn Days. Every month, when nobody was looking, she took a photo of Billy and sent it to the email address she had been given.

She had no idea where the Russians were keeping the scientist, but she felt satisfied that Billy was happy. The frightened little boy of three had turned into an energetic, enthusiastic and cheerful six-year-old.

One day she asked Neelam again how she would feel if Billy's parents were found.

"I'd be so excited for Billy," Neelam answered, hesitantly, "He needs his parents."

Mandy knew Neelam would be devastated if Billy had to be taken away from her. The old people loved Billy too, and he brought them endless pleasure. He accepted them exactly as they were and spoke to them all with a joy and innocence that Mandy found fascinating. Her own childhood had never been this easy. Billy was being cared for far better than *she* had ever been cared for by her mother and father. Had she actually done him a favour? Was he better off not having parents after all?

Chapter Twenty-five

England - the present

After Katie's visit, I started asking Gran to try to remember things. She remembers her son is Michael, but I can't get anything else out of her. She just looks at me blankly and then gets upset because she can't answer my questions, so I've stopped asking.

I'm glad Katie has been to Autumn Days and I don't know why I didn't tell her about it before. I'm actually very proud of my home and who I live with. Nobody else in my school has sixty-five people over the age of seventy to help them with their homework!

It's good to have Katie as a friend at school too. Jude is still trying his mean tricks on me, but they don't seem so bad now that it's three against two.

On Tuesday Jude tried to get me into trouble again. We were doing nonsense poetry in English and we'd all been told to write some silly lines on a piece of paper. That was easy, I just had to think of something Gran might say, so I wrote,

The owl's beak was inside out
The dog had lost its tail

I found a toaster on my nose
And put it up for sale.

I didn't think it was much of a poem, but it was definitely nonsense, and I smiled to think what Gran might say when I told her what I'd written.

Just as I finished, I felt someone push my chair forward and at the same time my piece of paper was brushed onto the floor. It was Jude.

"Oh Billy, so sorry," he gushed, grinding his muddy shoe into my poem, "I couldn't get past your big head."

"No problem," I said, "that was the rough copy."

Thursday came and Jude had a new and ingenious trap for me. I reckon he'd been planning this one for a while and he must have been fuming when it went wrong.

Our class had PE and as I went into the boys' changing room, I remembered I had one of Sid's socks in my locker and I told him he could get it out. As he pulled the door there was a twanging sound and something came flying out of my locker, past Sid's head and smack into the wall behind, leaving a big purple blotch running down the bricks and onto the floor.

The whole class stared at the stain on the wall and I ran to my locker. Someone had rigged up a catapult in my locker that would be triggered when the door opened. A balloon filled with thick purple paint had been attached. If *I* had opened the locker, I bet the balloon would've hit me in the eye. I looked at Jude and I knew it was him by the angry way he was throwing his kit on the floor.

A small riot erupted as everyone tried to work out what had just happened and who had made it happen. Mr Castle rushed in bellowing for us to be quiet. When he saw the stain on the wall, his face turned the same colour.

"If nobody owns up in five seconds," he fumed, "you will all stay in the changing room to clean up while I take the girls out for football."

There was a lot of grumbling because we all had to miss football. Jude had a double disappointment – missing football and missing me with the paintball!

On Friday, Mr Castle put up the football team for next week's match. Apart from missing the football lesson because of Jude's paintball, I'd been playing pretty well and thought I might be selected. Katie thought so too – she's always in the team and so is Jude.

After morning break, I ran down the corridor to see the team lists. The Under 13 team was up...and there was my name at the bottom of the list!

But my name had a line through it.

I couldn't believe Mr Castle could choose me and then cross me off! Did he think I'd put the paintball in my own locker?

I was really disappointed. So close to being in the team.

Katie was in the team and Jude was too. He kept coming up to me and murmuring the word, "loser" in my ear. At the end of the day I packed up my bag and walked out of school without even saying goodbye to Katie.

I had to pass the playing fields where Mr Castle was already getting the goal posts out for team practice. He looked up and saw me.

"Billy, where do you think you're going?"

"Home," I answered as rudely as I dared.

"Why aren't you getting changed for the practice?"

"Because I'm not in the team."

"You should have looked at the list. I've picked you for the match."

"I saw my name," I said. "But it was crossed off."

"Not by me," said Mr Castle, "You've got two minutes to get changed and be out here or I *will* cross you off."

I ran back into school wondering if Jude could have crossed my name off. As I went into the changing room, Jude was coming out and the look on his face gave me my answer. His eyes narrowed and he mumbled,

"Losers like you shouldn't be on my football team. There's no way I'm ever going to pass the ball to you."

I ignored him. He was the loser this week and I reckon he knew it.

****

I was feeling happy all day on Saturday. Gran's home, I found that my dad's definitely called Michael and I'm in the football team. On top of that Louis came to visit.

"Gran told Katie that her son is called Michael. At least I know his name for sure now," I said to him.

Louis looked surprised.

"Are you sure?"

"Yes, she often calls me Michael, but why are you looking at me like that? What was it you were going to say last time? About the fire."

"Billy, I don't want to get your hopes up, but the detectives on your case contacted me a few days ago about a possible connection."

"What do you mean?"

"When people go missing there is always a big search. It was very difficult in your parents' case because there were no names. The police didn't know who they were or where they had come from."

"And do they know now?"

"Not necessarily, but some secret information has been released from the British Space Programme, and it turns out a scientist went missing at the same time as your parents. They've tried to rule out various possibilities, but it could just be…

"That the scientist's name is Michael and he might be my dad?" I asked, hopefully.

"Not exactly. The missing scientist is a woman."

Chapter Twenty-six

England – three months ago

Mandy was sitting in her room looking at the three photos she kept in frames on the little table by her bed. In the first was Babushka, sitting in her rocking chair smiling and wearing the dragonfly brooch she had given to Manya.

"You can do anything you set your mind to and remember, I will always be proud of you."

Would Babushka be proud of her? Mandy was fairly sure her Grandmother hadn't expected her to end up working in a care home, but at least she'd been able to use the baking skills Babushka had taught her. She had been given the role of head chef after only a few years of helping out in the kitchen. It was a job she enjoyed very much, and her grandmother's recipe for blinis was a firm favourite amongst the residents.

The second photo was of Mandy's parents. She didn't particularly want to see the cold face of her mother, but it served to remind her that she mustn't end up like her, totally separate from the rest of the world.

She looked at her father with a pang of guilt. He had only wanted the best for her. She regretted not finding out more about him and about his family. Why had she not asked him about his work? Why had she not contacted him when he was dying?

She looked at the third photo which was of Billy in his school uniform. She thought back to when he had given it to her in the frame for Christmas.

"Mandy I'm not sure if you want this but Neelam said you might like it." he had said. "I had a few spare and I made the frame myself, out of an old cereal box."

Mandy had been surprised at her own reaction; she had burst into tears.

"I knew you wouldn't like it!" said Billy.

Mandy had to explain quickly that they were happy tears. She just couldn't remember anyone ever making her such a beautiful present before. She would put it next to her grandmother's photo, the most important person in her life.

"Not your parents?" asked Billy.

Mandy shook her head.

"Bit like me then," he said simply, and went back to sit with Gran.

It was soon after Christmas that Mandy had been forced to take her protection of Billy to a new level.

While Billy was small, Mandy hadn't had to worry about him too much because if he went out, he was always with Neelam or Louis. But when he was eleven, he went to a new school and Neelam agreed to let him walk by himself. Mandy had begun to imagine terrible scenarios where Billy would be walking home from school and one of the Russians would drive up in a white transit van, grab him and take him back to Russia.

So when Billy began walking to and from school, Mandy decided to follow him. She would put on a black tracksuit with a black hood and walk at a safe distance behind him. He never turned around and had no idea she was there. School was only a ten-minute walk, and it was easy to slip away from Autumn Days for the twenty-minute round trip.

One afternoon, Billy was late out of school and Mandy watched him turn left out of the school gates instead of right. Where could he be going? Immediately after Billy, a group of three other boys also turned left. They appeared to be following Billy. Mandy felt a shiver of unease and kept close behind them.

Suddenly Billy turned round to look at the boys.

"We're going to get you!" she heard one of them shout. Billy started running and Mandy wasn't taking any chances. She ran past the three boys to see if she could slow them down. With horror she watched as Billy stepped into the busy road. She heard the screeching of brakes and reached

Billy just in time to grab his arm and haul him back from the road. Luckily. he fell into a bush on the other side of the pavement. Mandy whipped round to face the three boys.

"Chto vy delayete?" she growled fiercely in Russian. "What are you doing?"

The three boys looked terrified and, as they ran off, Mandy had slipped out of sight before Billy managed to scramble out of the bush.

Mandy ran back to Autumn Days, worried that Billy might see her. She was fairly sure the three boys had gone, they seemed pretty scared. But Billy took longer to get home than she expected and she started to worry. She tried to busy herself with the lemon cake which had just come out of the oven and was relieved when Billy came into the kitchen. He had scratches on his face and leaves in his hair. She felt a surprising fury against the boys who had tried to hurt him and had an urge to take Billy's hands and tell him he would be okay, she would never let anything bad happen to him. But instead she offered him cake.

She stared at the kitchen door long after Billy had left the room. All these years at Autumn Days she had kept an eye out for Billy, but she was really just doing her job. Recently she had begun to enjoy Billy's company more and more.

He was so kind to Gran and the other residents, and she felt a need to protect him. She had to admit it, she had become very fond of Billy.

When it was time for Mandy to send the next photo of Billy to Russia she hesitated. Suddenly this whole procedure felt dirty, deceptive, cold-hearted.

She decided it was time to stop.

Chapter Twenty-seven

England - the present

"The missing scientist is a woman?" I repeated. "And she went missing at the same time as the fire?"

"That's right," said Louis. "Hopefully we'll get some more information soon but please don't get your hopes up Billy."

"Do you know the name of the scientist?"

"No, I'm afraid that's all the information I've got at the moment, but if we can find out she was married to a man called Michael and that she had a son, then we might be onto something."

That night I got out my secret book which I keep at the back of a drawer behind my clothes. It has all the theories of where my parents might be and why they haven't been able to find me.

- *They're dead.*
- *They offered themselves as scientific experiments to see if live humans could be frozen. They will be defrosted in fifty years.*
- *They're brilliant sailors who were shipwrecked and are now stranded on some desert island.*

The problem with my theories is that they don't explain the fire. I got a pen and wrote down a new idea:

- *My mum is a brilliant rocket scientist with a husband called Michael. She wanted to test the rocket she was working on and took my dad with her. They're orbiting the Earth on a ten-year mission and will be touching back down to Earth in the next few months.*

I suppose it's good that the police are still looking for my parents, but I wish they'd hurry up and find them. I've been waiting so long I don't really believe it will happen.

The next day was Sunday. Sunday is often the day when families come to have a look at Autumn Days to see if their elderly relative might like to live here.

I was sitting next to Frank and I saw Neelam come out of the lift with a family. There was a man wearing a denim shirt and tight, faded jeans which made him look as if he was permanently holding his breath. He had a long bit of oily hair plastered over his head. The woman was wearing a bright pink top and black jeans tucked into boots with very high heels. She had long yellow hair with pink streaks to match her pink mouth and nails. I wasn't sure if she was the man's wife or daughter, but she was holding onto his arm. Behind them was a boy. At first I couldn't quite see him because he was behind the others but as they came into the lounge I could see very clearly.

It was Jude.

Instinctively I jumped up and raced around the back of Frank's chair to hide. This was the last thing I wanted. I'd only just told Katie where I live, I'm definitely not ready for Jude to find out. This was terrible!

Of course Frank isn't the most subtle person in the world and he shouted, "Billy, what are you doing behind my chair?"

Luckily I had a chance to move behind the curtain which split the lounge area from the dining-room and Jude didn't even glance over.

Jude was dragging behind the man and the woman looking annoyed.

"Dad just give me the ipad, I'm so bored," he moaned.

"Derek would ya just give 'im the thing," said the woman. "Shut 'im up for a few seconds."

"No Cindy," said the man. "Did you hear what he said to me out there? He can't use words like that."

"But Dad," wailed Jude. "Why did I have to come?"

I thought Jude's dad was going to say something, but the woman pulled his arm and swished her long hair. She spoke through her teeth,

"Derek, this in't the time nor the place!"

As they walked past the residents, Beryl called out,

"Ooh look at those fancy pants. You'll enjoy living in this nuthouse!"

Neelam smiled apologetically at Jude's dad and ushered him and the high-heeled lady down one of the corridors.

Jude had hung back and was staring at Pascal who was doing some finger stretches and singing in French with his eyes shut. Jude changed his mind about staying in the lounge and wandered off down one of the corridors after his dad. But it wasn't the same corridor as the one his dad had gone down.

I didn't want Jude to see me, so I stayed where I was behind the curtain and was glad I had because he came back after a few moments. Beryl saw him. She pointed a finger at him and said, "You're a strange looking boy. Why is your nose upside down?"

"You're all crazy in here!" he said.

Then he went over to Gran. No way! I wasn't going to let him be rude to my Gran.

Gran was squinting at him as if she was trying to work out who he was. Then she said, "Thank goodness you've come, doctor. My baby has this

177

terrible rash, I think she's eaten too many strawberries. Would you mind taking a look?" and she held out her doll to Jude.

Jude seized Dardar by the foot and held her upside down before running around the room with the doll flying in big circles as Jude flapped his hands up and down. Luckily Gran couldn't see what he was doing as her eyesight is so bad and she turned to Mary and said, "That's my husband you know, he's so good with children."

Gran might not be able to see, but I could, and I was about to come out from my hiding place to confront Jude when Mary stood up. Mary appeared to be even more hunched over than usual and her lopsided face looked even more twisted. She slowly raised her head, and I was surprised to see she looked almost menacing.

On Jude's third circuit around the room he came face to face with Mary. He stopped abruptly and stared at Mary. I could clearly make out Mary's angry words, "Who's that trip trapping over my bridge?"

Jude was terrified. A sharp gasp escaped from his mouth and he dropped Dardar. Mary shuffled closer towards him. Jude turned and ran towards the lift. He desperately tried to press the buttons while twisting his head round to see Mary advancing on him. He frantically pulled and pushed the door making whimpering noises.

Mary had nearly reached the door and Jude looked like he was trying to press himself through it backwards. Mary went right up to him. It was too much for Jude. He opened his mouth and screamed a high-pitched howl. Mary just walked straight past him and as she did, I heard her say quite clearly, "Georgie Porgie ran away."

Jude sank to the floor in a heap. He didn't look like the tormentor who'd been bullying me over the past few months. I came out from behind the curtain and walked up to him. Jude looked up at me, tears streaming down his face.

"Billy, what are you doing here?"

"I live here." The words jumped out of my mouth. What was I thinking of? I had just told Jude that I live in a care home.

"You *live* here?"

"Yes I live here with these brilliant people. Frank over there is a war veteran, Pascal used to be a ballet dancer in Paris, and that's my Gran whose doll you nearly destroyed."

I listened to my voice. It sounded confident and firm. Was it even *me*?

Mary came back from her little walk.

"Keep her away from me!" stuttered Jude.

I took Mary's hand and she beamed at me.

"There came a big spider who sat down beside her and frightened Miss Muffet away!" she said.

"Mary," I grinned, "I think Jude has helped

you get your voice back!"

As I walked Mary back to her chair, I saw Jude walk slowly over to where Dardar was lying. He picked up the doll and gave it gently back to Gran.

Neelam appeared with Jude's dad and High-heels.

"Dad," called Jude "I think this place will be ok for Grandma."

Jude's dad looked at him. "You know what, Jude," he said. "I think you'd do better to keep ya mouth shut, nobody asked for your opinion."

"Yeah," said High Heels. "Why'd we care what *you* think?"

Jude looked down at the floor. I watched his dad slap his hand on the back of Jude's head before saying, "Let's get outta here before we catch something."

Neelam pretended not to hear and let them out through the coded door. I actually felt a bit sorry for Jude. I even glanced at him as the lift doors closed to smile at him, but his head was still down.

Perhaps having parents wasn't always such a good thing after all. It explained a lot about Jude.

Chapter Twenty-eight

England - the present

Mandy was having a lot of trouble sleeping. Over the past three months she had become more and more confused about her situation. Tatiana had already started putting pressure on her to continue sending photos of Billy, and Mandy had simply ignored them. But she couldn't ignore them forever. The one thing she was sure about was that Billy mattered, and she wasn't going to deceive him or Neelam any longer.

She wrote down a list of her options:

1. *Carry on as chef at Autumn Days and ignore Tatiana's threats.*
2. *Tell Tatiana I'm going to stay in England and want no further part in Goar V's operations.*

She looked out of the window at the rain and had another idea:

3. *Go back to Russia, find Feliks and give up this sham of a life.*

Things were becoming too complicated for Mandy and she wistfully remembered the day she had stood on the podium, winning the prize at school. What had happened to that little girl who had such a promising future? She was tempted to blame her parents, but she knew deep down she had made all her own choices. Now it was time to make another decision. She would find Feliks and see if he could help her relocate. Maybe she could go back to Russia and start again. She would miss Billy, Gran and Neelam, but she couldn't go on living a lie. Tatiana would certainly make things difficult for her, but it was time to move on.

Having made her decision, Mandy asked Neelam if she could take a few days off. Ken, the second chef could easily cover for her and she wouldn't be away for long.

She packed a small bag and headed for the airport.

****

Landing in Moscow, Mandy realised she hadn't been to Russia for nine years. Things had changed. The first thing that struck her was the new trains which whisked travellers away from the airport and on to other destinations. Then there were the cycle lanes. She had never seen so many bikes and she had to walk carefully to avoid being run over.

And where were all the kiosks? Last time Mandy had been in Moscow there were little stalls everywhere selling newspapers, sweets and groceries. In their place were burger bars and coffee shops cramming themselves into the spaces between jewellery shops and boutiques.

Mandy hadn't planned her trip very carefully. In fact she hadn't planned it at all. She had assumed Feliks would still be living at the last address he'd given her but that was seven years ago. He might have moved. She should have contacted him first.

She took a taxi to the place where she hoped Feliks would be living. A small town on the outskirts of Moscow. The taxi drove slowly down the street where Feliks' house should be, and Mandy looked out for number 23.

"Wait here please," she told the taxi driver as she jumped out of the car. It was getting dark and some of the houses had lights shining out through the windows.

Mandy stood on the pavement outside number 23. She could see into a room with two armchairs and a large sofa. There was a fireplace with some photos standing on the mantel piece, but she couldn't see clearly enough to recognise the people in them.

A man walked into the room. Mandy's heart leapt as she recognised her friend. He looked a bit heavier and his hair was shorter than usual, but it was good to see him again. She was about to go to knock on the front door when a small child walked unsteadily into the room. Feliks turned to pick up the little girl and as he did so another person came into the room. Karine.

Mandy stood still, transfixed at the scene in front of her. Feliks and Karine. And now a child. All the time she had been working as a cleaner and a chef in England she had supposed that everything in Russia would stay the same. But of course, it hadn't.

Feliks walked towards the window and, for a moment, Mandy thought he had seen her, but he simply lifted an arm to shut the curtains. Mandy's throat felt dry. This was not at all what she had expected, and she felt confused and disorientated. *So much for starting a new life in Russia with Feliks*, she thought. She dragged herself across the road to the waiting taxi and sank into the back seat.

"Where do you want to go now?" asked the taxi driver.

If only I knew, thought Mandy.

"Take me to the Novotel near the airport. Please."

In her small hotel room Mandy got the list of options out of her bag and crossed off number three. There was nobody for her in Russia and she didn't even feel she belonged here anymore.

She would make a new plan and go back to England in the morning.

After another sleepless night, this time in an uncomfortable hotel room, Mandy dragged herself out of bed. She went to the window. The streets below were grey, the buildings were grey and even the sky had grey clouds scudding across it. The scene matched her mood. As she tossed and turned in the night, she had come to the conclusion that there was only one thing she wanted to do now. She reached into the big pocket of her overcoat and pulled out the photo Billy had given her.

"I'm coming home Billy," she said, "and I'm going to help you find your parents."

There was a knock at the door.

Who could it be?

She checked her phone. It was off. But it hadn't been off when she arrived in Russia or when she had gone to find Feliks. With a sinking feeling she shuffled slowly across the room. Surely Tatiana hadn't traced her movements all the way from England to Moscow? Would she be standing on the other side of the door now, ready to rebuke Mandy for leaving her post? Couldn't they just leave her alone?

She put her hand out and slowly, cautiously opened the door.

Her eyes widened in shock, her legs buckled, and she sank to the floor...

Chapter Twenty-nine

England - the present

I didn't sleep that night because I kept going over and over in my head what had happened with Jude. I still felt odd on my way to school on Monday morning. Jude had been my enemy for so long and now he wasn't. I didn't know what to expect as I went into school. Yesterday, at Autumn Days I saw Jude as a totally different person. It was a bit like when you see a well-known actor playing different parts in different films. You see them as one person in one film and somebody else in another. I should know. It's always the same actors in the films I watch with the Oldies.

At school I took a deep breath and walked into the classroom. Jude was already there but standing slightly apart from his gang. He looked at me as if he had been waiting for me and he nodded his head. It was a tiny movement, but it told me things were going to be different from now on and I nodded back.

When Katie arrived, I told her about Jude's strange visit to Autumn Days.

"I felt a bit sorry for him," I said. "He has really weird parents and I don't think they liked

Autumn Days, so hopefully they won't come back."

Back at home that evening I went to talk to Gran as usual and that's when I noticed Mary's chair was empty.

"Where's Mary?" I asked Gran,

"Yes I looked in all the shops, but I couldn't find any curtains that matched," she replied, which didn't exactly answer my question. I sometimes wonder what Gran talked about before she had dementia.

Neelam appeared looking worried.

"Where's Mary?" I asked.

"I'm afraid Mary isn't at all well. The doctor thinks she's had another stroke and says she needs to stay in bed. She might have to go to hospital."

"Can I go and see her?" I asked. "She was in great form yesterday. She was even speaking properly. What happened?"

"Oh Billy, I wish I knew why these things happen. One day people can seem fine, even a bit better, and the next they can be really poorly. But go and see her, she would love to see you."

I went into Mary's room. She was lying in bed with her beads in her hands, running them through her fingers. I went up close and said, "Hello Mary. What happened? You were brilliant yesterday with Jude. He used to be my arch

188

enemy and because of you we're almost friends now."

Mary opened her eyes and smiled at me.

She reached out her hand and took mine. She squeezed it gently just like she always did, but this time there was a slight shake of her head. It was as if she'd had enough of being old, of not being able to say what she wanted to say, of everything being a struggle. I looked at her misty eyes and I had the strange sensation that they were telling me something. It was almost as though Mary was trying to say goodbye to me. I don't know why I thought that, but I waited quietly until she had fallen asleep and I crept out of her room. I looked back one last time and suddenly felt really sad. I walked slowly back to my room, sat on my bed and cried. I cried for Mary, for Gran and for all the old people who have to get dementia. The sad, confused and frightened people who were once proper human beings.

The next morning, I lay in bed and looked at the ceiling. I felt a bit empty.

I remembered about Mary being ill and I quickly got dressed and ran out to find Neelam.

Neelam's little flat is opposite my room. The door was open, and I could see through to her sitting room. She was standing with her back towards me looking out through the window. I knocked quietly and she turned around. Her face was sad.

"What's happened?" I asked.

"It's...oh Billy...I'm so sorry but Mary's gone."

"Gone where?" I asked, not wanting to hear the answer.

"I sat with her until really late last night and she didn't seem very well, so I called the doctor. An ambulance came, but by the time it arrived Mary had died. She fell asleep and just stopped breathing. She was very peaceful"

I couldn't speak. I had been right when I thought Mary was saying goodbye. Neelam took my hand and we sat on her sofa together. I felt numb. Other people had died at Autumn Days, after all most of them are very old, but never one of my special friends.

Neelam and I sat together for a long time.

When people die at Autumn Days, their photo is put in a frame and taken down to the reception area. I don't like it because sometimes I come back from school and there's a new photo. When Gran was ill, I was scared that I'd come home and see her photo in a frame. Now that Mary had died, I sort of understood why they do it. It's a sign that the person won't be forgotten. I asked Neelam if I could choose the picture.

"I want to find one of her wearing her red dress when she was 'the convincer'. Do you remember when she used to walk round with her clipboard?"

We both laughed. I was so sad that Mary had died but it felt good to talk about her and to think about the funny things she had done, and the good times we had. I would miss Mary.

Chapter Thirty

Moscow - the present

"Papa?" gasped Mandy as she sank to the floor.

"Manya, it's good to see you."

Mr Molchalin helped his daughter to her feet and led her to a chair inside the hotel room. He went to the door to check it had closed firmly before sitting opposite her.

"But Mama told me you were dead," whispered Mandy, barely able to speak.

"You know as well as I do that your mother has always suffered with serious mental issues. After you left home, she became more and more difficult to live with. I tried to persuade her to get help, but she refused. I tried to be patient, but she became aggressive towards me and I was left with no choice. I had to move out. I've been living in Moscow for the last six years."

Mandy closed her eyes tightly and opened them again. She must be dreaming!

"But how did you know I was here?" she asked.

"It's a long story. I want you to come with me. I've got something to show you. Pack your bag and meet me in the lobby. I've paid the bill."

And with that he was gone.

In a haze of bewilderment Mandy did as she was told. As she put her few belongings into her bag she tried to take in this strange turn of events. Why would her mother have said her father was dead and why did she believe her? All these years feeling bad about Papa and he was alive all the time. But if he was alive why hadn't he tried to find her?

Mandy didn't have time to ask herself any more questions. She followed her father out of the hotel where a large black Mercedes was waiting. The driver leapt out of the car and opened the rear door for Mandy. She slipped onto the cream leather seat next to her father who had got in from the other side.

"Whose car is this?" she asked.

"It's mine," said Mr Molchalin.

"Manya I've been waiting for this day for a very long time. Probably your whole life and now you must give me the pleasure of enjoying it. You will learn everything but in *my* time."

What is he talking about? Is he mad too? she thought, fearfully.

"But you were ill!" she exclaimed. "You were thin and pale when I left for England. I believed Mama when she said you had died."

Her father smiled, ruefully. "I was under a lot of pressure. Partly work and partly your mother's condition. My health improved dramatically after

I moved out."

"Your work?" questioned Mandy, "Why were you under pressure from work? You never told me anything about your work. You just told me you were an engineer."

"I couldn't tell you. And when you find out the truth you will understand why."

Mandy sat in silence. *What is this big secret? Where is he taking me?*

The car purred softly as it passed through the low, wooded hills on the outskirts of Moscow, over the dark, wide Moskva River and on towards the Presnensky District, where the buildings became taller, sleeker and altogether more impressive.

Finally, they drew up outside a tall, glass-fronted building. Mandy looked out of the window to see the words, 'DM Engineering' engraved into the glass above the entrance.

A man wearing a black suit and dark glasses stepped up to open the door for Mr Molchalin, while the driver opened Mandy's door.

In her jeans and sweatshirt, Mandy felt embarrassed and out of place outside the highly sophisticated and spotlessly clean building, but neither her father, the driver nor the man in the sunglasses seemed to notice.

She followed her father through the swing doors, into the building where a receptionist wearing a red jacket nodded politely and said,

"Good morning Mr Molchalin."

They walked straight through the grand entrance to a rectangular passageway with four lifts on either side. Another man, wearing the same red jacket as the receptionist, was holding the lift and he stood back to let Mandy and her father in. Mandy noticed her father didn't press a button for the floor he wanted. Somehow the red-jacketed man had known which floor he would be going to.

"Papa, what is this place?" asked Mandy.

"All in good time," said Mr Molchalin, mysteriously.

From the lift Mandy could see across Moscow. Higher and higher to the forty-second floor. The view was breathtaking. Mandy found herself being ushered out of the lift and into a large office with an enormous desk in front of a window with another spectacular view.

Mr Molchalin stepped into the corridor for a moment to speak to a tall thin woman with a very serious face.

"Zoran mustn't know. Did you get that message?" he asked, lowering his voice as if he didn't want Mandy to hear.

"Everything is in place," said the thin lady very quietly, glancing suspiciously at Mandy.

Mr Molchalin entered his office, walked around the desk and sat in the black leather chair behind it. He motioned for Mandy to sit opposite.

"I don't understand what this is all about," said Mandy. "Why are we here? Why do you have this huge office and why does everybody look at you as though you are so important?"

Mr Molchalin smiled at his daughter.

"I *am* important," he said. "This company is called Dimitri Molchalin Engineering. I have always been an ambitious man and I wanted you to be ambitious too. You showed so much promise at school. I wanted you to join me and maybe even take over the company one day." He paused for a moment. "And then you started to break away from me. You thought you could become independent. You believed you had chosen your own direction, didn't you?"

"I did," said Mandy. "I chose to go to University; I chose to study computer science and I chose my career."

"But *did* you choose your own career, Manya, or did it choose you?"

Mandy was confused. Of course she had chosen her own career.

"You don't even know what I did or where I went after university!" she protested, "I have always worked hard. You told me that I should make the Motherland proud of me and I have done my bit."

"Why did you come back to Russia?"

196

Mandy thought about Billy and about Feliks.

"I came back to find a friend of mine, and now I'm going home. But how did you find me?" she asked.

"All in good time, Manya," he said for the second time, provoking a prickle of irritation in his daughter. "Tell me exactly how you have helped the Motherland."

Mandy felt like a child. Here was her father, after nine years, trying to take control again; questioning her as if he had every right to know about her life. She tried to remain calm.

"There are certain things I need to repair and that is why I need to go home."

"And where exactly is home?" demanded her father.

"England." Mandy watched her father's face, expecting him to look surprised, but he continued smiling. It wasn't a friendly smile, it was a smug smile. As if he knew so much more than she did.

"I'm not sure going to England is a good idea for you right now," he said, and he leaned forward and pressed a button on his desk. "You can come in now," he said into a microphone.

There was a quick tap on the door and Mandy heard someone step into the room. She turned round and had the second shock of the morning.

"Tatiana!"

"It's good to see you Manya," she said.

Chapter Thirty-one

England - the present

It was Tuesday, a school day and I didn't feel like going. When I went into the lounge it felt different. I didn't like seeing Mary's empty chair and I spent the morning sitting with Gran because she didn't realize anything had happened. She chatted to me almost without stopping.

After lunch Neelam suggested it might take my mind off Mary if I went to school. She reminded me that I had a football practice. Mary wouldn't want me to be sad and she wouldn't want me to be dropped from the team because of her.

So I went.

We had football practices after school on Tuesday, Wednesday and Thursday. Mr Castle was so intense I didn't really have time to think about Mary. He made anyone who turned up late run an extra circuit around the pitch. Anyone not wearing the correct kit - an extra circuit. Anyone talking - an extra circuit. Sid was late, wearing the wrong kit and he was talking so he did three extra circuits.

The school team wasn't bad. We had a couple of set moves and although Jude wasn't being particularly friendly, he passed me the ball and even said that I'd made a decent pass. I don't suppose we'll ever be good friends but hopefully the dirty tricks and snide comments have stopped.

On Thursday evening I thought I'd better have one last football practice. Neelam told me to take down the mirror in the corridor in case I hit it and Pascal lent me his zimmer frame as a goal.

I put my Spurs kit on and walked onto the 'pitch'. I borrowed Dardar from Gran as my mascot and I held the doll's hand while waving to the capacity crowd at the same time. The stands were filling rapidly and even Beryl was asking for her wheelchair to be moved closer to the action. Beryl's a bit nosey and probably didn't want to miss an opportunity to make a rude remark.

"What's going on here?" she demanded.

"Welcome to Wembley, Beryl," I said. "You are about to witness the skills, the strength and the stamina of one of the best British footballers who has ever lived."

"So where is he?" she asked.

"It's me! You're going to watch me play football down the corridor."

"I'd rather eat my hearing aid," she said, and wheeled herself back to the TV.

199

Chapter Thirty-two

Russia - the present

Mandy looked from Tatiana to her father and back to Tatiana,

"You work together?" she asked, stunned.

"Of course," said her father. "Tatiana works for me."

"Manya, didn't you ever wonder how I knew all about you?" asked Tatiana.

"But I thought you were tracking me through the mobile," Mandy replied. "You said you could use my skills!"

"We *did* use your skills. We still need your skills." continued Tatiana, but your father had it all planned from the beginning. He employed me and the team that would become Goar V before you even left school. You should be proud of your father. He has masterminded an organisation in which you are a tiny cog. But he always wanted you to be part of it.

"The information you uncovered from Galileo was invaluable." said Tatiana, "And sending the photos of the child was an inspired idea. Galileo works for us now."

Mandy's thoughts flew to Billy.

"Where is Galileo?"

"I thought you might ask that," said Tatiana. "You must realise that we can't tell you. All we need you to do is to return to England for a few more months. The project is nearly complete and when it is over..." Tatiana paused for effect, "we will have no further use for Galileo or the child."

"What does that mean?" asked Mandy, feeling nervous. "What will happen to them?"

"Nothing will happen to the boy, so long as he knows nothing about us."

"And what will happen to Galileo?"

"That is not your concern, Manya," interjected her father. "Go back to England. Complete your task."

"Is he here, in this building?"

"He?" exploded Tatiana, "why would you assume Galileo is a man?"

"Galileo is a woman?" said Mandy. *Billy's mum is here!*

"Come with me," said her father.

"I don't think..." Tatiana tried to protest, but Mr Molchalin held up a hand to silence her.

"Careful Tatiana," he said sternly. "This is my daughter."

Mandy followed her father back into the lift and they descended a few floors. The doors opened onto a large, sterile looking room which was a hive of activity. Men and women wearing white coats, and masks covering the lower half of their faces were standing side by side, next to long white counters. A strange, sweet smell wafted into the lift making Mandy feel a little nauseous. A man wearing a white coat was about to enter the lift, but when he saw Mr Molchalin he retreated rapidly. Mandy noticed her father's face cloud over. He pressed the button for the lift doors to shut.

"What are they doing in there?" asked Mandy.

"That is a highly specialized laboratory. But that is not what I wanted to show you."

The lift doors opened again, this time onto a narrow corridor with glass doors on either side.

Mr Molchalin motioned to his daughter to follow him and he walked along the corridor, occasionally stopping to look through the glass into the rooms. Mandy looked too. Behind each door was a tiny room, each with a large computer on a desk. There was only one man or woman in each room, and they all had a greyness about them. As if they hadn't seen daylight for a long time. Mandy noticed that there were no windows in these rooms, just a simple bulb hanging from the ceiling.

"No nice view for these poor people then," ventured Mandy.

"View?" spluttered he father. "These are my

top scientists. I need them to concentrate, not be distracted."

He stopped again at a door, and this time quietly pulled down the handle. Mandy looked into the room as the person at the desk slowly turned her gaze to the newcomers. The woman was dishevelled, thin and sad looking. But something about her eyes gave Mandy a sharp jolt. She managed to disguise her gasp with a high-pitched, "Hello, this looks very...erm... interesting." The woman smiled weakly and turned back to her screen. Behind it, stuck to the wall, were some photos that Mandy recognised. She should do, she had taken them herself. The photos were of Billy.

Mandy stepped backwards out of the room stifling a sob. This was her fault. Billy's mum had been kept prisoner for nine years because of her. She had missed the best years of Billy's childhood whilst she, Manya Molchalin, had broken the poor woman's heart every month by sending photos of her son. In that split-second Mandy made the biggest decision of her life. She would rescue Billy's mum and return her to her son. It would certainly be difficult; it could even be dangerous. She clenched her fists as she turned to face her father.

Mr Molchalin was beaming down at his daughter.

"So now you have finally met Galileo. She has been an invaluable asset to the Russian Space Programme, and this is why I am so proud of you, Manya. You have certainly helped the Motherland."

Mandy nodded her head. She couldn't smile at her father and yet she needed to keep up a pretence if she was to have any hope of saving Billy's mum.

"I just want to get back to England and finish my assignment," she said.

"Manya I am proud of your dedication," said Mr Molchalin. "When you have completed your mission, you can return to Russia knowing that all this is waiting for you." He waved his arms expansively, as if he would be giving her the whole world. "You will be suitably rewarded."

Mandy took an afternoon flight back to England. She arrived at Autumn days on Thursday evening. Everything was the same. She breathed in the smell of washing powder and recognised Elvis playing on the juke box as usual.

Neelam was still up and she broke the sad news about Mary. It was yet another shock for Mandy and she was devastated. After the events of the past few days she was totally exhausted, and this last sorrowful announcement was too much for her. She went to her room, lay down on her bed and cried herself to sleep.

Chapter Thirty-three

England - the present

Friday. The Big Match.

One of the reasons I was so pleased to be picked for this match was because it's an annual event. My school, West Greenfield, versus St Peter's. The local Derby. Greenfly (us) against Bluebottles (them). The Year Nine match had been played last week and we lost 2·1. "A complete disgrace," Mr Castle called it. I think that's why he's so keen for us to win (he calls it getting revenge which I don't think our Head, Mr Granger would like as he says it's the taking part that counts).

In the last five years St Peter's has won four times. What makes it even worse for Mr Castle is that St Peter's coach is his brother-in-law.

This week in English we were learning the differences between bribery and blackmail. I could give some very real examples. During our practices Mr Castle has bribed us by saying he will buy us each a Mars Bar if we win. Extra Mars Bars for goal scorers and an extra one for Dylan if he saves all attempts at goal.

But Mr Castle started the week with blackmail by saying that if we lost we would all be staying behind after school to explain what had gone wrong. Sid and Dylan didn't like the sound of that and said they wanted to quit the team, so Mr Castle realised that bribing us with Mars Bars might work better.

All the players were allowed to leave their last lesson fifteen minutes early to get changed and have a last quick practice. Mr Castle was red in the face, his forehead all scrunched up and his legs all jittery. He was much more nervous than we were. When St Peter's arrived, he didn't go to welcome them, he just nodded crossly at their teacher, his brother-in-law, and beckoned for us to gather round.

Our team is mixed, but Mr Castle calls us *lads*.

"Right lads," he said, spitting the words out. "Remember all the work we've done this week. Keep the defence tight and don't let them near the goal. Forwards, once you've got the ball, sprint up and make sure to pass before you're tackled. Now get going and play your socks off!"

He was making us all feel a bit nervous now. I got into position and jogged up and down a bit. Slobbery Big Ben and Tyrone were on the side lines. Tyrone was wearing shades and had his hands in his pockets, trying to look cool. Big Ben had volunteered to look after the end-of-match doughnuts. It was a massive bag, but Big Ben seemed to be having a competition with himself to see how many he could cram into his mouth in one go.

I looked over to the car park where some of the mums and dads were arriving to watch the match. I blinked to check I wasn't dreaming. A big minibus had arrived and Neelam and Mandy were unloading three wheelchairs. I was really pleased that Mandy was back. I'm not sure where she went but I missed her. First out was Pascal, followed by Beryl and then Gran! Gran was going to watch me play football! They were all wrapped up, even though it was a warm, sunny afternoon. Finally, out clambered Frank wearing a Spurs hat and scarf. My Spurs hat and scarf! He waved at me and hobbled over to the side of the pitch where Neelam had set up a chair for him.

The whistle started the game and Jude kicked the ball back to Katie. I hoped she wouldn't pass it to me as I was a bit distracted by Beryl shouting from the side-line,

"Oh it's football. I thought it was going to be cricket! Take me home."

Katie did pass me the ball and I messed up by giving it straight to a Bluebottle.

"Crikey, it's worse than I thought!" shouted Beryl.

Frank was much more encouraging, even if he was a bit confused about the name of our school.

"Come on Billy! Come on Green Ones!"

The first half was a disaster. When the whistle blew for half time, we were 3-0 down. Dylan had done some great saves, but Mr Castle was furious. "What are you doing?" he shouted at us. "This isn't what we practised. Get back on that pitch and start playing football!"

It wasn't exactly a motivational speech and we all felt pretty useless as we took our positions. The other team were still sitting in their goal mouth eating oranges.

Beryl started singing *Happy Birthday* at the top of her voice.

I looked at our team. Everyone had hunched shoulders. As St Peter's sprinted back to their positions I heard Frank shout, "Come on Green Ones! You can do this, I know you can do this!"

I looked at Katie, "We can do this Katie!"

Katie looked at Sid, "We can do this Sid!"

Sid shouted back to Dylan, "We can do this Dylan!"

And so it went on, right around the pitch.

Their centre forward kicked the ball back to one of his team's midfielders and out of nowhere Jude raced forwards, intercepted the ball and dribbled it up the pitch. A quick pass to Katie who put it in the back of the net!

There was a loud whoop from the side-lines. 3-1.

Suddenly my team looked confident. So confident that we scored two more goals in fifteen minutes, one from Jude and one from Sid. 3-3.

Five minutes to go and I heard a new voice from the side of the pitch,

"Come on Billy mate, make it one more for me!" It was Louis.

Up until that moment I'd had no confidence. I hadn't had the ball much and although I'd made one or two good passes I hadn't got anywhere near to scoring. But now, with Frank still cheering me on, Mandy coming home, and Louis arriving to see the end of the match, I felt a surge of energy.

St Peter's had the ball and were dribbling down the pitch towards Sid. I sped down the wing and managed to get in a tackle. I could hear Frank cheering, "That's it Billy!"

Katie took the ball back up to the halfway line and passed to Jude. My legs felt suddenly light and I started to sprint forwards. Katie and Jude were up front on their own. I had to get there in time, Katie and Jude needed me. They did a quick little one two to get past the defence and then I was there. A short pass from Jude...

...everything went into slow motion. I heard Jude shout, "Put it in Billy!" but the ball was too far to the right, I wasn't going to reach it. I side stepped to get into position, took back my right foot and bam! Smack into the back of the net as the final whistle blew!

I was so surprised I fell over backwards. Jude was first to jump on me followed by Katie. Mr Castle rushed over and clapped me on the back. Then I was being held up in the air and the fans went wild (well I made the last bit up but that's how it felt.) I was a hero! Even Jude said the ball would have missed the goal if I hadn't been there.

Gran was sitting in her wheelchair bouncing Dardar up and down on her knee. She was very excited although I don't think she had any idea what was going on.

"Well done Billy!" said Pascal.

"What a goal!" shouted Frank.

Louis gave me a high five and went onto the pitch to congratulate the whole team. He looked at Jude and must have recognised him from the Safety Centre. "Glad to see your feet on the pitch are safer than your feet on the road!" he joked.

Mr Castle called us over, "Time to vote for man of the match," he shouted.

Frank started chanting, "Billy! Billy! Billy!" and Pascal joined in. Gran joined in too except she was shouting "Dardar! Dardar! Dardar!"

Mr Castle asked for some suggestions and I couldn't believe my ears when Jude said, "I think it should be Billy because he scored the winning goal."

And the rest of the team agreed!

"We're looking forward to our Mars Bars, Mr Castle." said Jude.

"M..m..mars Bars?" he stuttered, "Oh yes, good joke Jude."

"Well we won didn't we? You said we'd get Mars Bars and extra for the goal scorers," Jude persisted.

"Of course, of course. Yes, I'll make sure I get them soon," said Mr Castle, not very convincingly as he walked away.

"We're not getting any Mars Bars," muttered Jude. "He's just like my dad. Promises things that are never going to happen."

Chapter Thirty-four

England - the present

Mandy, exhausted though she was, woke early on Friday morning. Time was running out. Mandy remembered the day when she had first hacked into Galileo's diagrams. Tatiana had told her they were renaming the project 'Mantel' as a mixture of her name 'Manya' and the magnificent 'Telescope' they were building. At the time she had felt so proud and so valued. Now, she realised, it was just another of her father's whims. She could just imagine him saying to his workforce,

"We are going to name this project after my brilliant daughter!"

The thought made her feel sick.

When 'Mantel' was complete, her father would have no further use for Billy's mum, and she didn't like to imagine what that meant. Mr Molchalin didn't have any plans to send Billy's mum back to England, she was certain about that. And where was Billy's dad? There had been no mention of him at all, and Mandy was annoyed with herself for not having asked at the time. She had been too shocked about her own father and about seeing Billy's mum.

I don't want to go back to Russia, she thought. *I feel safe in England and I don't want to be part of Papa's world. If kidnapping people, forcing them to work and disposing of them is helping the Motherland, then it's not my Motherland. I want to be normal and to live in a normal place.*

The residents at Autumn Days were not necessarily considered normal by the outside world, particularly the ones who lived on the nostalgia floor, but since her trip to Russia, Mandy had changed.

It's not computers that give you purpose after all, she thought, *it's people.*

The people she wanted to be with now, more than ever, were Billy, Neelam and all the residents at Autumn Days. They had taught her friendship, empathy and compassion. And if she could bring them a small amount of pleasure in return through cooking meals and baking cakes for them, then that was her purpose right now.

As she lay in bed, staring at the ceiling, she wished she could forget about her father and Tatiana. She wished she could stay at Autumn Days forever. But she couldn't forget the look on Galileo's face. She, Manya Molchalin, was responsible for this mess and she would find a way to sort it out. She would rescue Billy's mum.

When Neelam asked Mandy to help her take some of the residents to watch Billy's football

213

match, she jumped at the chance. Just for today she would forget about Papa, Tatiana and the Mantel project, and she would enjoy being with the people who mattered. She had loved every second of the match. The old people shouting on the side-lines, the young people encouraging each other on the pitch. And when Billy scored the winning goal she had shouted and cheered with everyone else.

When she got back to her kitchen at Autumn Days, she decided to make a special meal to celebrate the football match, and she busied herself with recipe books. A meal that Billy would love, and she could finish it off with a big English apple crumble and ice-cream. She was totally unaware of the drama that was unfolding on the other side of the kitchen door.

Chapter Thirty-five

England - the present

It took a long time for Neelam and Mandy to get the Oldies back to Autumn Days. Louis took me in his car and was already on his second big slice of cake when the others arrived. I had told him every detail of the first part of the match and then we had analysed the last bit, especially the final goal!

As Neelam came into the lounge with Gran's wheelchair, the news was on TV. I looked up and saw a building on fire. Louis, of course, is always on the alert if there is any news about fire.

"... after many months of searching, police finally tracked him down to a disused schoolhouse on an uninhabited island in the Outer Hebrides. As the gang tried to escape there was a massive explosion inside the building. With no fire appliances on the island, fire-fighting helicopters were deployed to extinguish the fire. Further investigation has revealed three gas cannisters as the cause of the explosion."

I looked at the fire blazing on the island. I looked at Louis and then at Neelam. They were looking at each other and the blood seemed to be disappearing from both their faces.

"It's like the fire at my house!" I said, "Three gas cannisters. Is that what you were thinking too?"

"Yes," said Louis quietly, "I remember that night so clearly Billy. It was terrible."

"And do you think the people who started this fire on the news might be the same people who started my fire?"

"I wish I could give you an answer. I think we'll just have to keep an eye on the news."

Mandy had made a special meal to celebrate winning the football match. I tried to be enthusiastic about it, but I couldn't stop thinking about the fire and if it had some connection to my parents. I wanted to talk to Neelam and Louis about it, but they said it was best not to say anything in front of Mandy because she wouldn't understand what it was all about.

It was hard to sleep with all the thoughts in my head, and when I did sleep, I had a nightmare about Mr Castle bringing gas cannisters to school so that he could blow up the gym. Louis came in his fire engine and Gran was driving. Jude appeared and told me we had to score a goal or the whole school would burn down. It sounds funny now, but I woke up with my heart beating so loudly I thought I could hear footsteps and that

216

scared me even more.

At least it was Saturday, so I didn't have to go to school.

I went out to the lounge. Neelam was watching the news which was showing the fire on the Scottish Island again. Neelam turned it off as soon as she saw me as if she didn't want me to see it.

She sat with me while I had breakfast and I asked her lots of questions.

Do you think my parents were on the island? Have they caught the gang? Has the fire been put out? Is anyone still on the island?

She answered them as best she could, but I didn't find out anything new because she didn't know much more than I did. The only thing I found out was that the police had been looking for a man who had something to do with illegal drugs and it might have been his gang on the island. It was disappointing because I wanted it to be a man who was married to a missing scientist.

Gran was already up and sitting in her chair. I thought I might go and tell her about the fire and the gas cannisters to see if she had a reaction. It might jog her memory.

She was looking at an upside-down newspaper. A new carer who had just started working at Autumn Days kindly took the paper from Gran and gave it back her the right way up.

Gran took the paper and peered at it. I thought she might actually be reading it, she seemed to be concentrating so hard. Suddenly she started shouting, "Immerson! Immerson!" She became very upset and waved the paper around still shouting, "Immerson!"

Neelam rushed over and tried to take the paper but Gran wouldn't let her. I went to see if I could help but Gran was crying and shouting, and we couldn't understand what she was saying. I looked at the newspaper. The page she had been looking at had the headline *Scottish Drugs Haul* and two pictures. One was of the fire and the other was the photo of a group of men running. I'm pretty sure Gran couldn't read the small writing under the pictures, but I read it. Under one picture it said, *Abandoned schoolhouse ablaze*. And under the other it said, *Drugs gang fleeing the burning building*.

Was Gran remembering the fire? Might she be able to remember anything else?

"Gran are you alright?" I asked. She was gripping onto the newspaper and Neelam told me not to take it away. Gran threw it on the floor and put her head in her hands. "Immerson," she muttered as if she was in despair.

Neelam was so worried, she called the doctor. I was worried too, but I wanted to ask Gran what she was so upset about. I wanted to see if she remembered our fire. If she remembered my parents. Neelam said I mustn't mention the fire to Gran as it might upset her. She'd only just recovered from the last illness when she had to go to hospital, and she needed to be kept calm. I remembered Mary. I didn't want Gran to die.

While Neelam was looking after Gran I picked up the newspaper and tried to read the article. I'd never read a proper newspaper before and it was quite difficult to understand. I read that the police had been searching for somebody called a *drug baron* for nine years and they had located *suspicious activity* on the island. The police had arrived on the island too late. The gang had already flown off in a helicopter and the building had been destroyed by the fire. Undercover detectives posing as fishermen had taken the photo of the gang running away and had watched them escape in the helicopter.

Mandy came over to see why Gran was so upset and I gave her the newspaper to read. She wouldn't know about the fire at my house, but I didn't have time to explain right now because I wanted to ask Neelam what a drug baron was. She told me it's someone who controls an organisation dealing in illegal drugs. He buys drugs and then sells them to people. He doesn't care who he sells to. Sometimes young children are involved.

This was interesting but I couldn't see a link between the drug baron story and my missing parents.

Apart from two things:

1. The gas cannisters
2. Gran's reaction.

How could my Gran be involved with a drug baron?

The next morning there was a bit more information on the news. I found out that the police had searched the remains of the burnt-out building but had found very little. They believed the gang must have had a tip-off. Someone must have told them the police were on their way.

They showed a picture of the leader of the gang whose name was Zoran Krasnov. Zoran Krasnov was very dark, and I guessed with a name like that he might be Russian. It was all very confusing, and I was beginning to think Gran had made a mistake. She hadn't recognised anyone in the photo after all. I wished I could show her the photo again, but I was worried about upsetting her.

On Sunday afternoon I asked Neelam if I could keep the TV on the news channel so I could keep up to date with the drug baron story. I sat with Gran and tried to get her to do some 'mindfulness colouring'. Some of the Oldies like colouring but Gran isn't one of them. I couldn't get her to hold the pencils, so I started colouring the picture. Suddenly Gran started banging the arms of her chair.

"Babberchook Immerson! Immerson!" she shouted. I looked at the TV. It was the same photo of the men on the island running away from the fire.

"Gran," I said do you know one of those men? Is his name Mr Immerson?"

Gran shook her head violently, "Immerson! Im..mer...son!" she cried, pointing at the screen.

"But I don't know Immerson," I said, trying to keep calm while Gran kept banging her chair. The picture had gone and Neelam came rushing over. I stood up and went nearer the TV to try to hear what was being said. It was difficult with Gran shouting. Beryl had decided to join in because Beryl loves shouting.

"Why are you all shouting?" she shouted, "It's too noisy!"

It was too late. The news had moved to the next story and all the carers had come to sort out the chaos in the lounge. Neelam turned off the TV.

Gran knew one of those men, but who could he be? I found a Sunday newspaper and tried, for the second day in a row to understand it, but I couldn't find the name Immerson anywhere. It was all about Zoran Krasnov.

I asked Neelam if she would let me watch the news in her flat. I know she was worried about me getting too excited about the story, but she was more worried about Gran. The doctor had said it would be best to keep her quiet and calm. She was trying to make Gran comfortable in bed with a cup of tea and Gran was trying to get out of bed.

I thought it best to keep out of the way, so I stepped over to Neelam's flat and sat down on the beanbag in her lounge. I turned on the TV and waited. After about ten minutes the news came on and the first item was a man in a police uniform with the words *Scotland Yard* behind him. "We can now confirm that Mr Krasnov has escaped from an uninhabited island off the coast of Scotland," the policeman said. "He is believed to have flown with four other members of the gang to Moscow. Police are continuing to search the island." There was the same photo of the running men. The photo that made Gran so upset. I went to tell Neelam what she'd missed on the news. She was still with Gran who had calmed down and was half asleep. I spoke quietly so I wouldn't wake her up.

"Gran knows one of the men in the photo," I whispered. "She keeps calling one of them Immerson. Can I get the photo up online and show her again?"

"Billy we can't risk upsetting your Gran." Neelam whispered back, "She's too frail and you saw how distressed she became when she saw that picture yesterday."

"But what if it's something to do with my parents?"

"If it has anything to do with your parents, I'm sure the police will be in touch."

The police did get in touch a few days later but by then, with the help of Gran, I'd already worked it out.

Chapter Thirty- six

England - the present

When she served her special 'football celebration meal' on Friday evening, Mandy couldn't understand why Billy was so subdued. She thought he would be talking about the match, but he hardly spoke. She asked Neelam what was wrong, but Neelam was being a bit secretive, and as she cleared away the dishes, she wondered what had happened.

It wasn't until much later in the evening, when she looked at the news stories, that Mandy made the connection. A fire and an explosion caused by three gas cannisters. Surely it was a coincidence. Louis must have told Billy about the gas cannisters and Billy was upset because it reminded him of the fire when he was little. The story was connected to a drugs ring so it couldn't have anything to do with her father or DM Engineering, she thought.

The next morning Mandy had a headache. Her sleep had been disturbed by a nightmare in which she had made an enormous cake for her father. He had invited the tall thin lady from his office to share some of the cake but when she ate her slice, she started breathing fire and had set the whole building alight.

Mandy needed time to think but she also needed to carry on working; the residents were waiting for their breakfast. She made toast, porridge and scrambled eggs and when everyone had finished, she cleared it away. She was just about to start on lunch when there was a noise from the lounge. Somebody was shouting and crying. Mandy rushed out of the kitchen in time to see Gran throwing a newspaper to the floor and Billy jumping back in alarm. While Neelam tried to calm Gran down, Billy had picked up the newspaper and had spent some time looking at it.

Mandy asked Billy what the matter with Gran was.

"Oh, hi Mandy," Billy had said. "I'm not really sure. She was looking at this story in the paper and got a bit upset. You can read it if you like." Mandy took the newspaper and looked at the photo of men running from the fire.

With her heart thumping in her chest she walked as calmly as she could, back to her bedroom, clutching the newspaper.

She sat on her bed and looked again at the photo. She recognised one of the men. Where had she seen him before? Had he been to Autumn Days? Maybe he had delivered something. Had she seen him at her father's offices? She thought carefully but just couldn't place him. And why had Gran been so upset? Had *she* recognised the man too?

Mandy glanced down at her phone. At least there were no messages. Maybe the story had nothing to do with her father, and the man in the photo just *looked* like someone she had met before. She turned off the phone in the hope that if she cut the connection with Russia, the whole problem might go away. There couldn't be a link between this fire and her father. Gran must have been mistaken. Life could carry on for a little bit longer, and she would have time to work out how to rescue Billy's mum. That was the most important thing.

On Sunday morning the first thing Mandy did was to turn on her laptop to read the news. The Scottish story was the main headline:

Mandy read, "Police have named the Russian drugs gang leader as Zoran Krasnov..."

Zoran? I have heard that name recently, thought Mandy. *Zoran. Zoran.*

With a cry, Mandy leapt up. Zoran was the name her father had used at his office.

"Zoran mustn't know." he had said to the tall thin woman.

And then Mandy remembered where she had seen him before. Nine years ago he had slapped her face when she had pleaded with him to help save the baby in the burning house.

Things were even worse than she had imagined. It now appeared to be possible, no, probable, that her father's business extended further than the engineering firm he was so proud of.

She remembered the laboratory at DM Engineering, the strange smell, the look on her father's face. No wonder he hadn't wanted to see that particular floor.

"Papa has funded his enterprise with money from illegal drugs," gasped Mandy, almost inaudibly, to herself.

In a daze, Mandy went to the kitchen. *Just make the food, Manya,* she told herself. *Make everyone happy with a big chocolate cake.*

Half an hour later, Ken arrived to help with breakfast. He found Mandy turning out cake tins.

"Mandy, what are you doing? It's time for breakfast."

Mandy looked at him with a bewildered expression.

"Mandy, you don't look at all well," said Ken. I can manage by myself today, why don't you go and lie down for a bit."

Mandy didn't go to lie down; she went to the park for some fresh air. She hoped it might help to clear her head. She recalled the day, nine years ago, when she had walked round and round the lake in Lopatinskiy Park, trying to work out how to get back to England to find the little boy whose parents had been kidnapped. She had wanted to help him all those years ago but had not succeeded. She should have made more effort. Many hours later she returned to Autumn Days still not having worked out a plan. At least everything was quiet at Autumn Days, and Gran had already gone to bed.

Chapter Thirty-seven

England - the present

I thought about the situation. An evil drug baron called Zoran Krasnov had been discovered and the police had been looking for him for nine years. Nine years ago my house burnt down. Gran, who was in the house at the time of the fire, recognised someone in the photo of the drugs gang. If only Neelam would let me show her the picture again.

I had to go to school on Monday, but it was difficult to concentrate. I was expecting everyone to be talking about the fire on the Scottish island, but nobody mentioned it. I suppose not many twelve-year-olds watch the news.

The only good thing that happened at school was when Mr Castle gave our football match report, and I got a cheer when he said I had scored the winning goal.

At break I signalled for Katie to join me for a private walk around the playing fields. I told her about the fire on the island, the drugs gang and Mr Immerson.

"So you think your dad is a criminal? That's annoying. Just when you find your dad it turns out he's a drug dealer!"

"No Katie! He's not part of the gang. I think he was kidnapped on the night of the fire."

"I've heard about drug dealers," continued Katie. "My dad says they're evil and difficult to catch and everyone's frightened of them. They kill people. I'm surprised your dad's still alive!"

The conversation wasn't helping me. I was already worried about the whole thing and Katie was making it worse.

"I'm going to be a detective when I'm older," she said. "I'll travel the world arresting all the criminals and I'll start with Jude."

"Yeah, well I'm going to be a firefighter and save people," I said a bit crossly and ran off.

When I got home, I looked for the most recent newspaper and took it to my room. The front page had a picture of Zoran Krasnov, the drug baron and there was a long article about the drugs he'd been involved with. I searched for the name Immerson, but I couldn't find it.

I went back to the lounge to see Gran. She was half asleep. Her words had become very garbled since yesterday and she was even more difficult to understand than usual. I felt really bad about what I was going to do but I just *had* to know about Immerson. I checked to make sure that Neelam wasn't near and then I said in a sort of conversational manner, "Gran, do you remember a man called Mr Immerson?"

Gran looked at me. I was expecting her to get all excited again and was all ready to calm her down, but she just stared blankly at me.

"Immerson." I repeated.

Nothing.

Either Gran hadn't heard, or the name Immerson meant nothing to her.

Apart from showing Gran the photo again I just couldn't think of anything else to do. I went to find Mandy to ask if I could borrow her laptop. I couldn't ask Neelam in case she asked why I wanted it.

"Hi Mandy," I said, in a friendly way. "Could I just borrow your laptop for a moment, I need to find out something for homework?"

Mandy went straight to her room and brought her laptop out to me. I took it over to Gran, checked Neelam wasn't about, and then I googled the news story. There was the photo of the gang and, I hoped, Mr Immerson.

I tapped Gran's arm and pointed to the screen. She grabbed my hand and started pointing too. "Immycale! Chook Immycale!" she said, but at least she was calm. Now I was sure. Gran definitely knew the man.

"Gran," I said, "do you know that man?"

"Bah! Torso no im. Immerson!"

Suddenly I had a good idea. I grabbed a pen and a piece of paper and started writing down

Gran's words.

"That's great Gran," I said. "Who is he?"

"Immerson Immycale!" she said. She was quite calm and if anything, she said these last two words almost proudly.

"Immerson?" I asked.

"Nooo. Im mer son!"

I wrote it all down.

"Immycale?" I asked, trying to sound out the word just as she had said it.

Gran nodded. I think she thought I had finally understood. I hadn't understood and I found it very frustrating. But suddenly I realised how much worse it would be if you were trying to talk to someone and every time you said something that sounded perfectly clear to you, the person you were speaking to just looked at you blankly. Especially if it was something as important as the words Immerson and Immycale were to Gran. I hoped Gran would be able to speak properly again soon. It's always been a bit difficult to understand Gran, but since the Scottish island incident she's been talking gobbledegook (I learnt that word from Frank).

Neelam came over and Gran held my hand and nodded at me. "Immycale," she said.

Neelam looked at me and whispered, "Do you know what she's saying?"

"Not yet," I whispered back. "But I've written

it down and I'm going to work it out."

I looked back at Gran and she had fallen asleep, probably tired after all the excitement.

I took the piece of paper to my room and sat on my bed. I gazed and gazed at it. I made my eyes scrunch up. I read it upside down and backwards, but I just couldn't work it out.

That night I lay in bed saying the words in my head. Breaking them into small pieces.

Torso no im. Chook. Im mer son. Im my cale

Torso? That means body. And chook is what chickens say. So Gran saw a chicken's body?

I started again.

I my cul? My cul …. Michael!

It's Michael! I'd got it! It's my dad!

I looked again at the other words. How could I have been so stupid? No wonder Gran was upset. She wasn't saying Immerson at all. She was saying, "It's my son!"

Tors o no im. She was saying, "Of course I know him! Chook. Look!"

Of course I know him. Look. It's my son. It's Michael!

I jumped out of bed and turned on my light. 2.07am. I couldn't go and wake up Neelam in the middle of the night. I would just have to try to sleep.

My dad. My own dad. He's alive! What about my mum? Where was she? Had she been on the

233

island?

But how can my dad be part of a drugs gang? Has he been kept there as a prisoner for nine years? I had so many questions revolving around my head I didn't think I would ever sleep again, but I must have drifted off because when I opened my eyes it was light. My clock said 7:22. I rushed out of my room in my pyjamas to look for Neelam. She wasn't in the lounge or in the kitchen. I ran to her flat and knocked on the door but there was no reply. Now what?

I turned to go back to my room and noticed Gran's door wasn't quite shut. I quietly pushed it open and there was Neelam sitting on Gran's bed.

Gran looked very tired. She was shaking her head and patting Neelam's hand.

"Neelam, Gran's been trying to tell us that the man in the news is my dad!"

"What? No Billy, I don't think your dad can be Russian."

"No, not Zoran, Mr Immerson. But he's not Immerson. Gran's been saying, *It's my son!*"

"Are you sure?" said Neelam, "I'm going to call Louis."

Chapter Thirty-eight

England - the present

On Monday morning, it seemed to Mandy that things had begun to calm down. Neelam was rather preoccupied, but Billy had gone back to school and Gran appeared to have forgotten about the incident with the newspaper. Mandy took her a cup of tea and couldn't resist sitting with her to see if she could find out anything new. She asked if Billy was worried about something in the newspaper, but Gran's reply wasn't very clear.

"Imm baybel boo in chinder wind," she said.

Mandy had trouble understanding Gran at the best of times, but today her speech was even more slurred than usual, so she gave up. She didn't dare turn on her phone in case she had a message from Russia. She needed more time to work out a plan.

When Billy came home from school Mandy was pleased that he asked to borrow her laptop for his homework. This meant two things: firstly, Billy seemed to be carrying on as usual with school and homework, and secondly it meant he had no idea whatsoever about her involvement. *Nothing to worry about,* she kept telling herself as she went to the kitchen to mash potatoes and chop carrots. *Billy has forgotten all about the fire, everything is back to normal.*

When she woke the following morning, Mandy absent-mindedly turned on her mobile to see if there was any further information about the fire on the news. Immediately a stream of messages came through. She quickly scrolled up to read them.

Do not send photos until further notice.

This was followed by a whole string of urgent instructions which dated back to Saturday when she had switched the phone off.

Be prepared to pack up your things.

Do not discuss the Scottish fire with anyone.

Manya. Make contact now. This is important!

And then, finally, *Come home now!*

What should she do?

She sat upright on her bed, every muscle tensed, willing herself to think of a solution. Should she tell Neelam? Louis? If they told the police and the truth came out, she could be sent to prison. Should she tell Billy she had seen his mum? Tell him that she was alive and was desperate to see him? But then he might tell Neelam or Louis.

Another message came through.

Manya, are you there?

She ignored the message, but she knew time was running out. Her father and Tatiana must surely have something to do with the fire on the Scottish Island. Why else would there be such urgency to get her back to Russia. She got dressed and made her way towards the kitchen. She would have to hope Neelam would have the patience and understanding to listen to the whole story.

But Neelam wasn't in the lounge and nor was Billy. *Now what?*

Pascal was sitting in his usual chair and Mandy went to sit next to him. She asked if he had seen Neelam.

"Oui, of course," he said. "She has gone into her office wis Louis. Sey both seemed a little, how you say, flustered. I have no idea what it is all about."

This was not what Mandy wanted to hear. Once again, things were spiralling out of her control and she didn't know what to do about it.

At nine thirty, Mandy took a phone call from Mr Granger who wanted to know why Billy wasn't at school. Worse than she thought – Billy hadn't gone to school!

She crept towards Neelam's office to try listening through the door. She could hear the muffled voices of Louis and Neelam. *What could they be talking about?* Mandy knocked and opened the door at the same time, hoping to learn more but Neelam and Louis both stopped talking abruptly and waited for Mandy to speak. Neelam told her to tell Mr Granger that Billy wouldn't be in school for a few days.

What's going on? Why isn't Billy going to school?"

Then Billy came to the door to reassure Mandy. The words he said did not reassure her in the slightest.

Chapter Thirty-nine

England - the present

Neelam fetched her laptop and got up the news photo again. She held it in front of Gran saying, "Is your son in this photo?"

Gran looked very closely. I think she knew this was something important and she took a long time looking. I could hardly stand it. *Come on Gran,* I was thinking, *point to him!*

Finally Gran pointed to the same man as before, "Immerson, yes, i Michael. He's a doctor you know." These last words came out quite clearly.

"Yes Gran!" I shouted, I couldn't help it. Gran had done it! I thought about what she had just said. So now I might have a doctor dad and a scientist mum. Why wasn't I the cleverest boy in the school?

Gran was smiling and looking very proud. She kept looking at the picture, putting her head on one side and then on the other.

"Is that my dad then?" I asked. "Nooo," said Gran, shaking her head and laughing as if I'd said something ridiculous. "Im my *son*!"

Gran must have forgotten the connection between *her* son and *my* dad. But at least she was laughing. I like it when Gran laughs.

Neelam phoned Louis immediately to tell him what I'd found out. She agreed that Gran recognised the man in the photo, but she said to remember how confused Gran gets and I mustn't get too excited. It might just be someone who *looks* like my dad.

I believed Gran. She had recognised the same man three times and just now she looked so proud when she was pointing at the photo. I really hope my dad isn't involved with a drugs gang. Maybe he was kidnapped and has been held hostage on the island for nine years. But where's my mum and why wasn't she in the photo too? I felt tired and I couldn't work out the puzzle. Neelam told me Louis was on his way. Maybe he'd be able to solve the problem.

Before Louis arrived, I wrote down all the clues about my parents. It wasn't much but it was more than I had before:

My mum is possibly a scientist who was kidnapped and taken somewhere, but not the same place as my dad.

My dad is a doctor (if Gran got that bit right) and was probably kidnapped by a Russian drug baron who took him to live on a Scottish island for nine years. Now the gang have taken him to Russia.

It all seemed a bit hopeless and I had no idea

how they could be found.

When Louis arrived, Neelam took us into her office and shut the door behind her.

I told Louis everything I'd told Neelam. About how I'd worked out what Gran was saying and how she'd recognised my dad in the photo.

Then Neelam and Louis started talking about things, but I couldn't follow what they were saying. I sat on the swivel chair thinking about the first thing I would say to my parents if they come back.

"Hi Dad, do you support Spurs?"

"Hello Mum, do you use bunsen burners for your experiments?"

I couldn't think of anything that sounded normal.

Then Mandy knocked on the door to tell Neelam that Mr Granger, the headmaster, had called wanting to know why I wasn't at school. We had all completely forgotten that it was Tuesday. Neelam asked Mandy to tell Mr Granger I wasn't ill, but I might not be in school for a few days. When Mandy left the room, she forgot to shut the door behind her. Louis indicated to me to shut it and I found Mandy still outside the door. I think she was trying to listen. I felt a bit sorry for her not knowing what was going on, so I mouthed some words to her, "It's okay, Mandy, my dad might have been found."

She gave me a funny sort of smile, but I bet she's happy for me.

Louis asked me to sit with Gran for a bit. It was just an excuse; he really wanted a private chat with Neelam.

Gran was asleep but Frank wasn't. He was sitting in his usual chair reading the paper.

"Come over here Billy lad," he said. "What's going on with this hush-hush stuff and your Gran getting all hot under the collar?"

"Have you heard about that explosion on the Scottish island?" I asked, and Frank nodded. "Well Gran recognised my dad. He's one of the men in the photo."

"Not one of those blinkin' Russian druggies?" he said.

"No! The druggies have been holding him hostage. He might have been there for nine years and now Louis and Neelam are trying to work out how to get him back."

Frank suddenly sat up straight and turned the newspaper on his knee upside-down. He couldn't have made it more obvious. There was something he didn't want me to see.

"Frank, is there something in the paper you don't want me to see?" I asked.

"No no no, nothing at all," he mumbled, too quickly.

"Frank, if there's something new, please let

me see."

"I don't think you should read it just yet, lad. Maybe we should wait until they find out who it is."

"Who *who* is?" I asked and put out my hand.

He slowly handed me the paper and I turned it over. The headlines jumped out at me:

Body Found on Scottish Island.

I felt hot and cold at the same time. A body - that meant a dead person. I tried to read the rest of the article, but Frank was talking, and I couldn't concentrate.

Louis came out of Neelam's office and I showed him the headline. He looked as shocked as I felt. He sat next to me.

"Billy mate," he said, "This doesn't mean anything until we get more news."

"But couldn't the body be my dad?" I asked.

"Let's not jump to conclusions. One of the detectives on the case is coming to see us this afternoon. Maybe he'll be able to give us some answers. Let's just stay positive and see what he has to say. He's bringing some photos of the island and he wants to talk to Gran. Look, why don't we go to the park? We could take the football."

I didn't feel like playing football, I wanted to read what it said in the paper.

"Thanks Louis but I'll just sit with Frank for

a bit."

"That's okay, I'll go and get us all some coffee and biscuits. I think we could do with a bit of a boost," said Louis and he went towards the kitchen.

I still had the newspaper and I tried to read the article again.

"Billy, I'm not sure it's a good idea to..." Frank began, but I interrupted.

"Frank, I need to read it," I said, and he held his hands up as though he knew there was no point in arguing.

I read the article, but it didn't tell me much. I wanted to know where exactly the body had been found. Whether it had been a man or a woman, and how the person had died. I desperately needed to know if my dad was okay. The paper didn't answer any of my questions.

Louis came back with the coffee.

"Mandy's behaving strangely today," he said, "I went into the kitchen and she left straightaway. Have I done something to offend her?"

"She's a blinkin' Russian isn't she. Unpredictable," said Frank.

"You've got to stop talking like that," I said. "You sound racist. Mandy's a good person."

Straight after lunch I went down in the lift

with Neelam, Louis and Gran. We were going to meet the detective in one of the private rooms where relatives can talk without being disturbed. After a few minutes, the detective came in and he wasn't what I expected. I thought he'd look like one of those cool policemen you see on the TV, but he wasn't cool. He had his hair stiffly gelled back and his trousers were too short.

"D.C. Watham-Jones," he said, shaking hands with Louis. He nodded at Neelam, but he didn't look at me or Gran.

"Now then, I understand someone has recognised one of the…"

"Excuse me," I said to DC Watham-Jones because I couldn't wait any longer. "But do you know who the body is yet?"

DC Watham-Jones looked at me as if he hadn't noticed me before.

"And who might you be?" he asked in a condescending voice.

"I'm Billy, and I need to know if it was my dad."

"Well young man," he said. "Do you honestly think I'm at liberty to reveal that sort of information?"

I wanted to say something rude, but I felt Louis' hand on my back, so I kept quiet.

"Now who is the person who *thinks* she recognises a suspect?" said D.C. Watham-Jones.

"Hang on a minute," said Louis. "The man Gran recognised is *not* a suspect."

"We'll see," said D.C. Watham-Jones with a smirk, and I liked him even less. I wished they'd sent a different detective.

He held up a black zipped folder and took out some photos. He placed them on the table in front of Gran, and Neelam gave Gran her glasses. I felt a bit tense because it was really important that Gran should recognise my dad again, but she seemed to be more interested in the detective's bright yellow tie.

"Well?" said D.C. Watham-Jones to Neelam as if there was no point asking Gran herself, "Does she recognise anyone?"

I went round the table to have a closer look at the photos. They weren't the same as the photo in the paper and they weren't as clear. I could see five men, but I couldn't be sure if they were the same five men.

"Gran," I said. "Can you see Michael?"

Gran looked at me and smiled. Then she pointed at me and said, "Michael, there you are."

"No Gran, I'm Billy. Can you see Michael in the photos?"

"This is pointless," said Watham-Jones, and by now I *really* didn't like him. "She can't recognise her own grandson. How can anyone expect her to pick out a man she hasn't seen for

246

nine years."

"Detective Constable Watham-Jones," said Neelam in her calm voice, which always meant trouble. "Gran recognised the man in the news photographs on several occasions. If you want further assistance from her you will need to find some better photographs." And with that she wheeled Gran out of the room.

Louis and I looked at each other. Things were not going well but we still hadn't seen all the photos. There were plenty more in his folder.

"Could we see the other photos please?" I asked.

"You can have a look, but you won't find anything of significance," said Watham-Jones, handing them to Louis.

Louis gave me a pile and we both started looking through. Most of the photos were of burnt-out buildings, a couple were of a path which seemed to be heading towards a beach and quite a few were of burnt pieces of paper with writing on them. I couldn't find any others showing people. Louis handed me one of the photos from his pile. It was of a burnt piece of coloured paper and he was pointing at a tiny blue shape in the middle of it. I took it and examined it. It was the logo of the Spurs cockerel! I looked at Louis, but he had gone back to examining the other photos. I looked at DC Watham-Jones, but

247

he was busy on his phone.

I could tell immediately that the cockerel was on a Spurs second kit from a couple of years ago because the background was light blue, and I've got one exactly like it. I thought it was odd that a Russian drug baron would have the Spurs away kit! Maybe it was my dad's shirt? How good would it be if we supported the same team!

Then I noticed a sort of flowery pattern at the edge of the paper. It was just like one of Gran's dresses. As I examined it more carefully, I saw that it *was* Gran's dress! I knew this for certain because right at the very edge of the burnt piece of paper was a tiny hand. Dardar's hand. It was the photo Manya had taken of me and Gran on my tenth birthday.

What could this possibly mean? How could a photo of me have ended up on a Scottish Island? I must have looked surprised or something because Louis said, "What is it mate? What have you seen?"

I looked at DC Watham-Jones. I wasn't about to tell that fruitcake anything.

"Nothing," I said. "It's just the buildings. They're so badly burnt."

What I was actually thinking was how on earth a photo Mandy had taken of me have ended up on a Scottish island where my dad happened to be? This was weird and I wanted to get out of there and talk to Louis. Alone.

"Louis can we go now?" I asked, taking one last look at the photo.

Louis jumped up and led me out of the room. He turned to DC Watham-Jones saying, "Just see yourself out."

Louis led me out of the room, out through the front door of Autumn Days and all the way to the park. We didn't speak at all until we were sitting on the bench that looks out over the lake.

The lake was the same as usual and so were all the people in the park. A little girl was feeding the ducks with her mum. There were joggers, cyclists and walkers. I wished I could go back to the day when I last came here with Louis and we'd played football. Everything had become so complicated.

On the way to the park I'd been trying to work out if Mandy could have sent my photo to a Scottish island. I know she's Russian but surely she isn't involved with a Russian drug baron!

"Louis," I began. "That piece of paper on the photo. I recognised it."

"What do you mean?" said Louis.

"It's a photo of me and Gran."

"What? How do you know?"

"It's the one Mandy took. I've got it in my room. How is it possible?"

Louis didn't speak for a while. He was trying

to work it all out. After a few minutes he said, "I had a feeling there was something fishy going on with Mandy. Let's get back and ask her what she's been up to."

I was relieved. I thought he might want to tell the police first, and then that idiot Watham-Jones might come back.

"We don't want that idiot Wally-Jones to come back do we!" said Louis, which made me laugh and I felt a bit better.

Chapter Forty

England - the present

Mandy couldn't decide what to do. Billy and Louis were sitting with Frank most of the morning and Neelam was busy with the residents. If Mandy confided in her, Neelam would definitely tell Louis, and Louis might go to the police, without letting her explain herself.

Messages were still coming through on her phone from her father and Tatiana telling her to go back to Russia. She knew she would have to respond.

"Where is Galileo?" she texted.

"That is not your concern. You need to come home for your own safety," came the response.

"Who is Zoran?" she tried.

"A liar and a traitor. Not your concern."

None of it made sense. Zoran was a liar and a traitor? More determined than ever to help Galileo, Mandy sent a final message.

"I'm staying here." She turned off her phone.

After lunch she watched as Neelam pushed Gran in her wheelchair towards the lift. They went down with Louis and Billy. She ran down the staircase and got to the bottom just in time to see the four of them disappear into one of the meeting rooms. A few minutes later a man with gelled hair and trousers that were too short came through the front door. He marched up to the reception desk and said in a loud voice,

"DC Watham-Jones. Louis is expecting me."

Mandy watched as DC Watham-Jones was shown into the meeting room. Behind her there was a flurry of excitement amongst the residents.

"What's a detective constable doing here?" asked one elderly lady.

"Ooh I don't know but I think Billy's in that room with Louis," said her companion.

"What's it all about then?" said the first.

"I don't know but I'm not going anywhere until I find out!"

At that moment, another visitor swept through the front door and Mandy froze. Tall and dark with long strides and a thick Russian accent. *What was he doing here? Why had he come?*

She turned on her heel and ran back up the stairs to the Nostalgia floor just in time to hear the phone ringing in Neelam's office. She backed away, knowing that the call would be for her, to announce the arrival of her father.

Ken was passing and picked up the receiver, "Yes, she's up here," he said into the phone, "Mandy, there's someone in reception asking for you. Mr Molchalin. Can they show him up?"

Mandy had to think quickly. Why was her father here? He must have already been on his way to England this morning when she received those messages from him. He had come to take her back to Russia. She must *not* go down to him; she was safer up here where he wouldn't be able to force her to go with him.

Her only option was to invite her father to come upstairs. She asked Ken to show him which way to go.

As if in a trance, Mandy made her way to her room. She straightened out the cushions on the armchairs and arranged her two remaining photos.

"Babushka, I really need your help," she said to the image of her grandmother.

There was a knock at the door and Mandy went to open it.

"Manya, how are you?" said Mr Molchalin in English, using a friendly tone for the benefit of Ken who was standing next to him.

Mandy ushered him into the room and quickly shut the door. She motioned for her father to sit down but didn't speak. She was afraid her voice would reveal her terror.

"Manya, you need to know the truth. Then you will understand why you need to come home. You will *want* to come home."

Mandy nodded and sat down.

"When I met your mother, she was a smart girl, straight out of school. She had no ambitions other than to look pretty, get married and have lots of children. I was a few years older and needed a wife who was willing to stay at home, accompany me to business functions and start what I hoped would become a Molchalin dynasty. Your mother fitted the bill perfectly. She even came with a willing cook and baby-sitter."

"Babushka." said Mandy, softly.

"That's right," continued Mr Molchalin. "But after you were born, your mother was not able to have more children. She was devastated. She went completely to pieces, but I could see, from the day you were born, that you were a fighter. You kicked and screamed your way through the first few weeks of life, and I decided to make you my protégé. I didn't need a dynasty, all I needed was one child of my own who could learn from me, and eventually take over the business that I was, already very successfully, building.

"You showed so much promise, Manya, you were everything I could have hoped for. But then you began to have your own ideas and started drifting away from me. I wasn't discouraged. I believed your strong-will could be shaped and, without you realising, I could lead you to the destiny I had always planned for you."

Mandy wanted to cover her ears and run away. Had her father really been controlling her life all along? She looked at Babushka's face smiling at her out of the photograph,

"You need to be strong. You can do anything you set your mind to," she had said.

I am not strong, thought Mandy, *I have done exactly what Papa wanted. I am a weak, worthless puppet, completely under his control since the day I was born.*

Mr Molchalin's voice interrupted her thoughts.

"Tatiana helped to guide you through university, but you were so easy to lead, Manya. You wanted to serve the Motherland just as much as I did. We are so similar, can't you see?"

"No, Papa," said Mandy, finding her voice. "I can't see. I would never take parents away from their child. I would never blackmail them in the way you have blackmailed Billy's mum. I am not ruthless like you."

"But Manya," exclaimed her father, "it was you who led the team to Galileo. You found her, maintained contact, and enabled us to capture her. It was your idea to send the photos. Ultimately you are the blackmailer."

He's right, thought Mandy, horrified. *It was me all along. I am just like him.*

"And now I'm going to take you home and we

255

can work together. You and me, Manya. We can take on the world!"

"Who is Zoran?" Mandy asked, suddenly remembering the story on the news."

"Zoran is no longer part of my team. He is nothing. I don't need an imbecile on my team. The man managed to blow up his own brother!"

Mandy tried to take in what he was saying.

"But he's taken Billy's Dad!" she cried.

"I assume Billy is the child. Why are you so concerned about him?" asked Mr Molchalin, "He's not family. He's not your problem."

"But I am *his* problem," said Mandy, "I have caused all his problems and I need to solve them. He is a sweet, kind, innocent child, and if there is any good in me at all, it is because of Billy. He has shown me how to care about other people. And now he needs his parents. You must send them back to England."

"It is true that I still have Galileo. She has been a tremendous help to my project. Those photos you sent every month were enough to persuade her to co-operate."

Mandy tried to hold back a sob. How could she be related to this monster?

Her father continued. "I have no idea where the father might be. Zoran held onto him from the very start. And now he has set up on his own. He deceived me."

"You led me to believe your business was engineering," said Mandy. "But it's more than that isn't it. It's funded by illegal drugs!" she said, almost crying with rage.

"To create an empire like mine, one needs money," said her father. "Lots of money. If a few feeble, impressionable individuals choose to destroy themselves by taking illegal narcotics, it is a bonus. The world is all the better without them."

Be strong! urged Babushka from her photo. *You are not like him. You are a better than him.*

"I am not coming to Russia to work with you, Papa! I am staying here in England with my friends."

Mr Molchalin stood up and took a step towards Mandy's chair. He towered over her and Mandy flinched as her father lifted his arm.

There was a light knock at the door and Mandy was aware of someone entering the room.

"Mandy, are you in here? I have *got* to talk with you *right now*, it is really, really important."

Mandy pushed her chair back and ran towards the figure at the door, but he pushed past her and went further into the room.

"Oh hello," he said. "Are you Mandy's dad? You look just like her."

Mr Molchalin looked astonished at this stranger who had burst in on them. The stranger faltered for a moment before putting out his hand. "Nice to meet you, I'm Billy."

Chapter Forty-one

England - the present

Louis and I arrived back at Autumn Days and as soon as the lift opened on the Nostalgia floor, Neelam rushed towards us to ask how we got on.

"Louis will tell you," I called to her as I went into the kitchen to find Mandy.

She wasn't in the kitchen. I hoped she hadn't gone out and walked quickly towards her room. I knocked on her door and opened it. It was a bit strange because Mandy rushed towards me and I could see a man standing behind her. I ducked past Mandy to get a better look at the man. I couldn't remember her ever having a visitor before. I could tell immediately that he wasn't English. It might have been his long black shirt or his dark bushy eyebrows or his grey beard, but then I saw that he looked just like Mandy and words popped out of my mouth,

"Hi. Are you Mandy's dad? You look just like her,"

I was a bit flustered because the man looked angry so I thought I'd better be polite and I stuck out my hand to shake his, because I'd seen Louis do that when he meets new people.

"Nice to meet you, I'm Billy," I said.

Mandy came to stand next to me and told me it *was* her dad, but he was just leaving.

"No no, Manya," said her dad, calling her Manya which surprised me. Maybe it's Russian for Mandy.

"No, I'd like to meet Billy. I've heard about you," he said, looking at me.

"Oh," I said, wondering if Mandy had sent photos of me to her dad as well as to the drug baron.

I don't know what it was about this tall man that made me feel suspicious, but I didn't trust him. I wondered if he had anything to do with my parents.

"Mr Molchalin," I said, hoping I'd got his name right. "Have you come with news about my parents? I want them back so badly. I can't even remember what they look like and...and...I need them..." Then I started crying and I was so embarrassed I couldn't say anything else.

Mandy's dad left. He just walked to the door and left. He didn't say anything, not even goodbye and I thought I'd made a terrible mistake. Maybe he'd just come to England to visit his daughter and I'd come in, a complete stranger behaving like a total nutcase.

Then I remembered the photo.

"Mandy, you know the Scottish island on the news? Well the police found a piece of paper with

260

a photo of me on it. It was there on the island. It was that one you took of me and Gran, the one in my room."

Mandy's face changed lots of times in the next few seconds. First she looked shocked, then thoughtful, then worried and finally really sad. She told me she was sorry because she had been very wicked. She had told me lies and done very, very bad things. She said it was time to tell me the truth. I couldn't understand what she was talking about.

Mandy made me sit on her bed. She started to tell me she was a Russian spy. A Russian spy! The only thing I knew about Russian spies was from a James Bond film called, *From Russia with Love*, which is one that the Oldies sometimes watch. I've never really understood what was going on in it, but Mandy didn't look much like the film's Russian spy who didn't wear many clothes a lot of the time. She's just Mandy, the cook at Autumn Days Care Home. I was trying to take it in when Neelam came to the door.

"Billy, what on earth are you doing in here? I've been so worried. I didn't know where you'd gone."

I was in a bit of a daze. A Russian spy? I was still trying to picture Mandy jumping into a speed boat, holding a gun.

Then Mandy told Neelam she needed to talk

to her too and that it was very important.

"Well I suppose I could spare a few minutes if it's that important," said Neelam. "Sarah can hold the fort for a bit. But I must tell Louis that you're in here."

"Is he in here?" It was Louis. "Billy, mate, I've been worried about you. Don't go hiding like that. Why are you in here anyway? What's Mandy been saying to you?"

Mandy asked Louis to come in too. She said we *all* needed to hear what she had to say.

So we sat in Mandy's room and she told us everything she'd done. I could hardly believe what she was saying. She'd been working for the Russian spy team that set fire to my house, but then she'd felt bad about my parents being kidnapped and came to live here, at Autumn Days, to watch over me. She was the mysterious figure who'd pulled me out of the road and frightened Jude away. She'd been sending photos of me to my mum in Russia to persuade her to keep working on a big telescope project. She supposed the team must have sent the photos to my dad too, but she said she didn't know he was being held as a prisoner on a Scottish Island. She told us she had no idea there were drugs involved, she thought she was helping her country to win some race in space.

Mandy knew about the body on the island too.

It was Zoran Kraznov's brother. By now I was totally stumped, but I do remember thinking that even though it was pretty bad for Kraznov's brother, I was so relieved the body wasn't my dad. Neelam, Louis and I just sat there staring at Mandy. She has lived here all this time and none of us had any idea about who she was and what she was up to. I don't know how long it took for Mandy to tell us her story or how many questions we all asked but it was dark when she finished and none of us had noticed.

I was exhausted. I hadn't slept well last night and now it was late. I felt angry with Mandy for pretending for so long, but at the same time I knew she had done what she thought was best for me. My head felt like one of Louis' weights and my brain wasn't functioning, so I went to bed.

I had another bad dream. I was stranded on a tiny island with Gran and Neelam when a boat came ashore. A man who looked a lot like Mandy's dad got out and ran up to where we were sitting. He took hold of one of my arms and Neelam took the other. The man said he wanted to rescue me and only had room for one person in his boat. Gran was shouting, "Michael, Michael save me!" and Neelam wouldn't let go of my arm. There was a big explosion and I found myself in the middle of a fire with Russian drug barons dancing around the outside looking like devils.

They were going to turn me into powder and sell me to addicts.

I woke up sweating. It was still dark, and I wished it could be morning with everything back to normal.

Then I remembered what Mandy had told me and I knew that things would probably never be normal again.

Chapter Forty-two

England - the present

When Mandy had finished telling her story it was late. After Billy had gone to bed Louis wanted to call the police straight away but Neelam stopped him.

"Louis, you've had a very long day and we need to discuss what is best for Billy. Mandy has told us the truth and I believe her when she says she is going to do everything she can to get Billy's parents back. Let's just wait until morning."

Reluctantly, Louis had agreed, and they left Mandy alone in her room.

Mandy wasn't intending to sleep. She had one chance left and she couldn't afford to make a mistake.

All night she sat at her laptop writing ideas of what to say to her father and how to persuade him to send Billy's mum home.

During the night she received a message from her father.

Manya this is your last chance.

Tatiana would do anything to take your place beside me.

I will give you until midday tomorrow.

If I don't hear from you by then, you will no

longer be my daughter.

Mandy wanted so much for it to be over. To be cut off from her father forever was her greatest wish. Did she dare ignore him and set herself free?

At six o'clock Mandy looked at her clock and realized she'd been up all night. There was a faint knock on the door. It was Billy, still in his pyjamas looking tired and confused.

"Mandy," he said, "you are the only person who can get my parents back for me. Please, please make it happen."

Mandy knew he was right. She was the only person who could get Billy's parents back and there was only one way to do it.

Chapter Forty-three

England - the present

As I was on my way to the lounge to sit with Gran, I overheard Neelam and Louis talking in Neelam's office.

"We should go to the police," I heard Louis say.

"We've already discussed this," replied Neelam. "You know why we can't."

"But we need to follow the official channels," he argued.

"Not this time, Louis. This is Billy's only chance. Do you really want that Watham-Jones involved in *this*?"

I heard Louis murmur something about getting in touch with someone higher up as soon as he got back.

I tried to work out what they were talking about and where Louis was going. It seemed that Louis wanted to go to the police, but if he did Mandy could be in big trouble, especially if it was the idiot Watham-Jones. If the police took Mandy away there would be no-one to get my parents back. I was still thinking about this when Mandy came out of her room carrying a big suitcase. It made me feel a bit panicky because if she was going somewhere how would she be able to help me? If she was going back to Russia it could be dangerous for her, but if she was leaving Autumn Days because she was frightened of being arrested, I knew I would never get my parents back. She was my only hope. I was about to ask her where she was going when she started saying goodbye to the residents. They didn't understand what was going on any more than I did.

"A little silk scarf with dat outfit would be parfait, non?" Pascal said.

"If you're leaving, let me give you some advice," said Beryl. "Now this is important so listen carefully. You mustn't start dying your hair until you're at least thirty-two."

Frank looked at Mandy, then he looked at her suitcase. He just grunted and went back to his newspaper.

Gran put out her arms for a hug and I noticed tears in Mandy's eyes as she pulled away.

Neelam told me to get my shoes on and be ready to leave.

"Where are we going? Do I need to bring anything?" I asked.

"Billy it's complicated and we need to hurry. Let's just get going and I'll explain everything later," she replied.

We went down in the lift and came out on the ground floor. It didn't seem right that everything seemed so normal downstairs when my insides were looping the loop. Louis was waiting in his car by the front door and Mandy was sitting in the back. I got in next to Mandy and she smiled at me. Neelam sat in the front. I couldn't work out where we were going, and everyone seemed so serious I didn't think it was the right time to ask questions.

Suddenly Neelam spoke and it made me jump.

"Billy, I think you need to know where we're going," she said. "We're going to the airport and if everything runs smoothly, we will be collecting..."

"Don't get his hopes up," interrupted Louis.

"I just think Billy should know," said Neelam. "The thing is, Billy, we're hoping your mum will be coming home. We're going to the airport."

My mum? My mum might be coming home? Suddenly everything changed from being very strange to being totally unreal. I looked out of the window to see if we were flying, then I'd know I was dreaming. But through the window I could just see other cars driving along next to us. Louis is a careful driver so plenty of cars were overtaking us. There was a big four-by-four with a family who looked like they were jumping all over the car. They couldn't have been wearing seatbelts so I knew Louis must be distracted because he would definitely have made a comment about the dangers of driving without a

269

seatbelt if it had been a normal day. The car behind the four-by-four had an old couple in it looking miserable. It was just an ordinary day for them, and I felt like winding down my window and shouting to cheer up because my mum was coming home. I wanted to shout it to the world!

"My mum," I finally managed to say, "how is this happening?"

"We don't know for sure that it *is* happening yet," said Louis, looking across at Neelam. "We mustn't get too excited. It's just a chance."

So my mum *might* be coming home. Today! I *might* see her, but I might not. I couldn't work it out. How could they not know for sure, and why was Mandy in the car with her suitcase?

I tried to think logically, taking one piece of the puzzle at a time but I still couldn't work out where or why Mandy was going with her suitcase. She'd only just come back from a visit to Russia so why would she be going again?

Then I started thinking about what it would be like if my mum was really coming home. It was only yesterday that I'd found out my dad was alive, but yesterday felt like a year ago. And now it could be my mum who's coming home. Getting my parents back was what I'd always wished for. Now part of that wish was coming true and I should be feeling excited. But I wasn't feeling excited, I was feeling sick because I was so scared. I was scared for myself, but I was even more scared for Mandy because I didn't know what she was going to do.

I thought about Mandy, Neelam and Louis. Gran, Frank, Beryl and Pascal. Autumn Days. My whole life. It would all have to change if my mum came back. My mum won't want to live in an old people's home!

Who would teach me history like Frank? How could Pascal help me with French? What would happen to Gran? Would she have to stay at Autumn Days without me? Louis wouldn't be able to pop in to visit and eat cake with me. Mandy's cake.

And Neelam. She's been my mum for nearly nine years. How can I turn around and tell her, "Well thanks Neelam but my mum's come back so I don't need you anymore"?

I looked at Mandy. She took my hand and gave it a squeeze and I was shocked to see that she was crying and trying not to let me see.

"Are you going back to Russia?" I whispered. "You don't want to live in Russia, you told me."

She nodded her head and turned away, wiping her eyes and taking deep breaths. She flinched as the sound of a message came through on her mobile. I kept my head pointing forwards, trying not to show that I had noticed, but I was looking at her out of the corner of my eye. She read the message and covered her eyes. She was still holding my hand and her grip became tighter. I gripped tighter too, hoping it might comfort her.

We sat there like that for a while but then she seemed to relax a bit. She turned to me with a smile and reached into the big pocket of her coat. She took out an envelope, looked at it for a moment and then handed it to me. It had my name on the front. I was about to open it when she gave a little shake of her head and put her fingers to her lips. She wanted me to open it later.

Chapter Forty-four

England - the present

When they arrived at the airport, Louis' car didn't take the route that passengers usually take. He took a side road that led away from the big car parks and the passenger terminals. He was still unsure whether they were doing the right thing. If Billy's mum didn't arrive, he feared they would never get her back. For nearly ten years Billy had been such a big part of his life and this was a moment they had discussed and imagined many times, not really believing it could ever come true. He carefully followed the signs for 'private passengers', driving slower and slower. He glanced in his rear-view mirror to see Billy's strained expression and said a little prayer. If Billy's mum wasn't here today it would do him more damage than if she had never been found. Billy needed his mum to be on that plane and in a few minutes they would find out whether she was coming home.

Louis stopped the car at a barrier and showed the special code which had been sent to his phone earlier that morning. Mandy handed over her passport. The guard checked everything carefully then he nodded and raised the barrier to let the car pass underneath. Another guard waved the car forward towards a small parking area. Louis looked around at the private jets parked in neat rows. Was she in one of them?

Mandy let go of Billy's hand and quickly got out of the car. She needed some air before she broke down completely. The message on her phone had felt like a conclusion. An ending that she didn't want and yet she had brought it about. She just wanted this last bit to be over as quickly as possible.

Neelam, Louis and Billy had also got out of the car and were standing in an anxious huddle, not knowing where to look. Suddenly the cabin door of one of the planes swung open and the steps were slowly lowered. Four pairs of eyes fixed on the exit door and the group watched, hardly daring to breathe as they waited to see who would emerge.

****

From the top of the steps a small pale woman peered out into the brightness. It had been a long flight but far from feeling tired, her heart was pounding in her chest as her gaze swept over the scene in front of her. A group of cars were parked a couple of hundred metres away, and next to them she could see people waving: a dark, athletic-looking man, a slim woman wearing a floral dress, a younger woman holding a suitcase and a boy who was jumping up and down, both arms flailing in the air so wildly he was in danger of falling over completely. Cautiously, the woman walked down the steps, hardly daring to hope this could actually be happening. She stood at the bottom of the steps waiting for instructions. It had been nearly ten years since she had been allowed to do anything of her own free will, and she didn't want to make a mistake now.

Neelam felt a lump rise in her throat. So this was it. Ten years of being Billy's mum was about to come to an end, and all she could do was watch. She tried to distract herself by smoothing down her skirt and twisting her hair around her fingers, but when she looked back towards the plane and saw the small woman standing at the bottom of the steps looking fragile and lost, Neelam felt nothing but sympathy. Here was the woman who had been taken away from her child and had missed all those precious years. At least she could be confident that she was handing over a wonderful boy who was kind, friendly and happy. And she knew that whatever Billy did and wherever he went, a small part of him would be hers forever. She smiled and joined in with the enthusiastic waving.

Mandy felt her limbs become heavy, as if they

were refusing to co·operate. The text she received in the car had told her that the jet carrying Billy's mum had landed safely. Billy's mum appearing at the top of the steps was the sign that the deal was almost complete. Now all she had to do was to keep her side of the bargain and she knew what was required. Billy's mum would not be released until Mandy boarded the plane.

She steeled herself for what she had to do and managed to express a few final parting words of gratitude and affection to Neelam and Louis. Then she looked at Billy and hugged him tightly. Neither of them said a word, but words were no longer necessary. They both understood.

Mandy walked across the wide stretch of tarmac to the plane, exchanged a few words with Billy's mum and then, very gently, nudged her towards her son.

Mandy climbed slowly to the top of the steps, looking back to watch as Billy and his mum ran towards each other.

As they stood together, locked in an embrace, Billy turned his head. It seemed, to Manya, that he was looking straight at her. She shivered involuntarily, despite the heat from the aircraft's engine.

Billy lifted his arm to wave to the Russian girl who had both shattered his life and restored it.

Mandy turned and entered the cabin of the

small plane. She paused for a moment.

Is this it? She wondered. *Is my life in England over? Will I ever see him again?*

The sound of footsteps made Mandy turn back. It was Billy's mum. She approached tentatively, almost shyly as if she didn't know what to say. Then, with a sob, she stepped forwards and wrapped her arms around Mandy, holding her close.

"Thank you so much, Mandy," she said, releasing her gently, "I owe you everything. Please find Michael and come back soon. Billy needs you."

Mandy watched as she walked back towards Billy who was still smiling and waving. She took a final deep breath before stepping into the aircraft. *This needn't be the end; this could be the beginning.*

"Don't worry," she murmured in Russian, *"I will definitely be back."*

THE END

Epilogue

Mum is brilliant and I didn't need to worry about anything at all. She wants to live at Autumn Days with the rest of us for now, and certainly until Dad is found. She knew a few things about me from the photos Mandy sent. Mum said it was the photos that kept her going all these years, knowing that I was safe and happy.

On the way home, Neelam explained that the only way Mandy's dad would release my mum was if Mandy went back to Russia. Like a swap. We could have my mum if he could have Mandy. I know how much Mandy wanted to stay in England, and how much she didn't want to go back to her dad. She had done the swap for me.

When we got back to Autumn Days, I couldn't wait for Gran to see Mum for the first time. I didn't think Gran would recognise her after so many years, but as usual, Gran gave me a big surprise. She looked at Mum and said straightaway,

"Hello Megan, that was a long walk! Did you remember to buy bananas?"

Mum and I have a lot to talk about. I want to know all about her, about Dad, Gran, my family and about me! But first I want to open Mandy's letter.

Dear Billy,

I am not wanting to go in Russia. Not one little piece. But I must do this now.

When I am back to Russia it will be very difficult for me in contacting you and impossibility to tell you all that is happening. Somebody will be spy on me surely and listens to all my conversations and checking all my message. It is everything I am deserving because it is what I once was doing to other people.

Papa promised in help to find Zoran, but I cannot trust him. It is coming difficult finding your papa and it will take some long time, but certainly what I am going to do.

Never will I stop looking for him. Never.

I want to come again in England and when I come I will to return to you your papa.

For now, you will have much enjoy with your mama.

You are lucky with living the best people I am ever meeting. I have learning so much but, most of everything it was you, Billy who is teaching me being kind.

I am very sad for all the terrible bad things I made for you and your family and I hope, one day, you will be much forgiving me.

Sorry for bad English. I write never a lot since this language.

For now, until we see once more,
До встре́чи!

Mandy x

About the Author

Caroline has a dynamic (his word) husband, four fantastic daughters, a fabulous son and a special dog called Nelly.

A part-time teacher, tutor and writer of children's books, she also plays hockey and tennis when her right leg allows.

Subscribe to Caroline's blog and find out how she became a writer and what inspires her.

www.carolineboxall.com
Instagram: caroline_boxall
Facebook: Caroline Boxall

Look out for Caroline's picture books about Ace spy Charlie and his cousin Annie as they travel the world to stop the bad Baron Quill.